A TIME TRAVELER FROM THE 20TH CENTURY IS IN A DESPERATE race against time across 11th century England in an attempt to change the course of history. But which history? And which 20th century? With chilling overtones of the environmental crisis facing us today, but incorporating the latest scientific thinking about the Multiverse, John Gribbin offers a unique blend of real science and adventure fiction.

Old fashioned hard Sf at its best—all the science in the story is real, even the time travel. It just hasn't happened yet—*or has it?*

John Gribbin is best known as "the master of popular science writing" (Sunday Times), with over a hundred non-fiction books to his credit. But his science fiction output, which includes *The Sixth Winter, Innervisions* and *Double Planet,* has also received critical acclaim. He has returned to writing Sf in 2009 after a gap of more than ten years, bringing to his new works of fiction much of the science that is making headlines in the 21st century.

Dr John Gribbin is a Visiting Fellow in Astronomy at the University of Sussex, a Fellow of the Royal Society of Literature, and a long time fan of Buddy Holly. His next novel, *The Alice Encounter,* will appear from PS in 2010.

TIMESWITCH

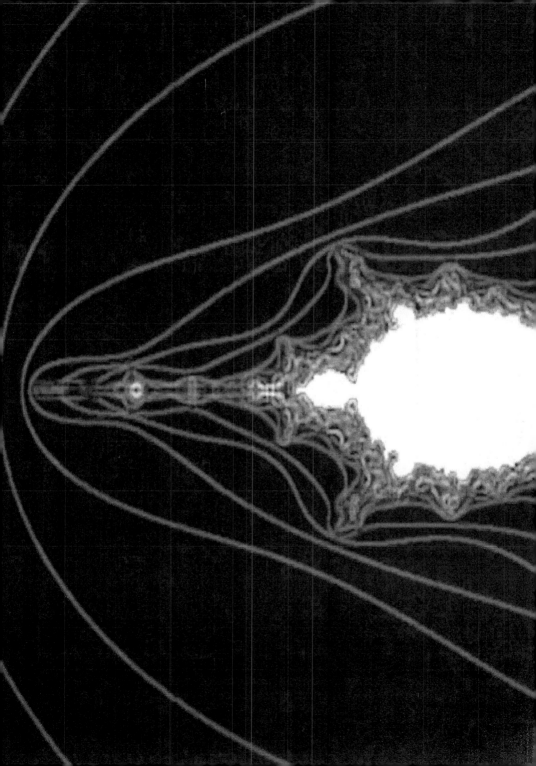

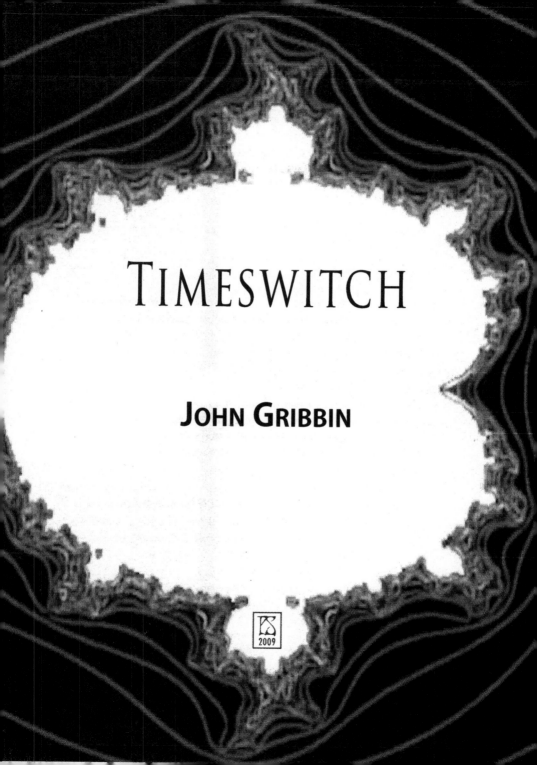

TIMESWITCH

JOHN GRIBBIN

2009

This one is for Dave Garnett, who insisted that it wasn't a short story; also for David Compton and Ben Gribbin, who suggested improvements.

All the characters and events portrayed in this story are real; they do not, however, necessarily take place in the same reality that you inhabit.

1966 JUNE 22; 10.23 AM

On the dusty Salisbury plain, there was no sign of life except for a few shrubs and some scorched grass. The Sun beat down, relentlessly, from the blue, almost cloudless sky. High above, a lone bird circled, scanning the plain for any carrion on which it might feed.

In the underground chamber, all was quiet. Concealed lighting maintained a soft glow, but there was nobody there to benefit from it. The door was closed; in the middle of the chamber, the Portal stood, waiting.

ONE

THE HELICOPTER TILTED ON ITS FINAL APPROACH TO THE Plains Research Centre, giving Jan Ricardo a good view of Sarum, where the tall spire of the great cathedral dominated the centre of what was now an essentially abandoned city, occupied only by a few monks. The contrast with Winchester, still nominally the capital of England and of the English Empire, from which this short hop had commenced, was striking. There, a few vehicles still moved in the streets, and from the height the helicopter cruised at a casual observer might have thought he was viewing a bustling community, full of life. Such a casual observer would not have remarked on the absence of pedestrians; it was, after all, full daylight, when nobody would venture out without protection. Only the expectant eye could have caught the dilapidated state of some of the buildings, the absence of any traffic at all in the streets out from the old centre. Winchester itself was now a capital on paper only, with government, both king and parliament, long since gone north, to Glasgow, where the air was cooler and the rains were more reliable. But Sarum was a city in decay, the crumbling state of the buildings obvious even from this height, and the few tracks of wheeled vehicles in the streets serving only to emphasise the thickness of the dust in which those tracks had been made.

As the machine levelled up for landing, Jan looked across the parched brown scrub of the plain. Nothing seemed to have changed during his short leave in York; there was no outward sign of the turmoil that must be going on within the Complex. A few low, twisted trees were dotted here and there; part of the Environment Ministry's half-hearted attempt to combat erosion and desertification. The limited extent of their success in holding back the desert could be gauged from the swirl of dust that rose around the helicopter as it swooped low over the tree tops in a flashy landing manoeuvre and touched down, rocking slightly as one skid grounded before the other, almost in the shadow of the great circle of stones.

He waited as long as he dared, hoping for the dust to settle, gauging the distance to the low building that, he knew, contained the entrance to the underground chamber. Well, he was paid to take risks; it was nowhere near noon, and, looking on the bright side, the dust in the air might help to protect him from a bad case of instant sunburn. Couldn't keep them waiting, after all. Checking that the wraparound sunglasses were secure, he pulled the loose hood of his lightweight jacket over his head, nodded to the pilot of the machine, opened the door and jumped down. Hands plunged deep in the large pockets of the jacket, he strode briskly, being careful not to run (no point in letting the guards think he was chicken) into the building. Before he was quite under cover, the whine of the helicopter's engine increased once more, and he felt the patter of dust against his hood, which fluttered in the downdraft from the rotor blades. *Bloody show-off pilots*, he thought.

MacNeil was waiting for him by the desk, but they still had to go through the routine of identification—pass, thumb print, voice, the usual stuff—before the guards would admit him. Not much point, really, if what he'd heard was true. But they had to keep up appearances, perhaps even more than ever, now. Nobody wanted to be labelled inefficient when there was a major security alert in operation and an intruder in the Complex, even if the intruder had been caught. MacNeil was studying him carefully throughout the procedure. He was OK, for a Scot. Stickler for the regs, but OK. Jan grinned at him.

"Well? Am I me?"

MacNeil frowned. "You're you, all right. We haven't had you out of sight since you were picked up in York. And we won't. You're under constant surveillance now, Ricardo. Whatever's going on here, you're the key."

"Is he that much like me?"

MacNeil took him by the arm, steered him away from the guards, down the main corridor. "Not really. Similar, but there are differences. Oh, he might pass for you to an acquaintance, or in a crowd, but he'd never get through Security. That's what makes it so puzzling. Why bother with an imperfect impersonation? And how *did* he get in here? Security's records say they're clean, and that computer is supposed to be tamper proof. There's one more person in this complex than there ought to be, and that person is enough like you to pass without comment in the corridors. I don't like it."

"And he's sticking to his story?"

"You haven't heard the half of it. He's been very well briefed. Somebody knows far too much about this project. But if they know *that* much, why do they need a spy? With what he's already told us, they could go public and blow us apart. We'd never get approval before the Portal closed again."

"Suppose he's telling the truth?"

They stopped outside a door. MacNeil looked him square in the eye. "Now, *that* way, Ricardo, lies madness. If he really is you, and he's from 1968, *two years* in the future, and he's done what he says he has done, then you've already carried out the Project, and failed. Unless, maybe, you noticed fields of wheat and birds singing in the trees on your way in here today? Don't even think about it."

"So you're sure I won't disappear in a puff of gamma rays when I shake him by the hand?"

"You've been viewing too much cheap science fiction. Besides, you're not going to shake him by the hand, just yet. We're saving that little surprise for later. Come on."

He opened the door, led Jan into an observation room. The old-fashioned one-way glass along the wall to the left was augmented by a full sound and vision system, giving a view of the room next door from a point in the top corner of the wall opposite the glass, which, of course, showed as a mirror in the life size display on the opposite wall of the observation room. The result was that the observers could see everything that went on next door, most of it from two angles, while a sufficiently naive subject just might think he could find a corner out of sight from the one way window, and do whatever it was he might want to do when he thought he was unobserved.

There was a shadowed figure in the room, back half turned to the door, facing the glass wall. In the darkness, his face reflected, ghost like, in the glass as Jan moved to stand behind him while MacNeil shut the door. It was Matt Evans, chief scientist in the project. Matt and Jan went back a *long* way; after all the hustle of the past few hours, it was comforting to see him. For a moment, though, he didn't move, and Jan, looking over his shoulder, saw the intense concentration in the reflected eyes, as Matt studied the man in the next door room. The eyes were cold, calculating; the face set in a mask of concentration. Jan had seen that cold concentration before, when Matt was absorbed in a difficult scientific problem. Nothing, he knew, would deflect his friend from the path to a solution to the problem in hand. *I'm glad he's on my side of the glass,* Jan thought. *Pity the poor bastard in there if Matt's got any plans for him.*

Then Matt turned, smiling, to greet them. The concentration was gone from his face, eyes lively and alert as he extended his hand. For a brief moment, this was the Matt Jan knew, and liked, best—the one who could charm birds out of trees, and funding out of tight-pursed government departments. But the flash of charm was short-lived.

"Hi Jan. You made it. No point in me hanging around here; I'll see you once the Chief has brought you up to speed. Take care."

With a nod to MacNeil, he was gone before Jan could respond. That was Matt in business mode, all right. No time for unnecessary social graces, even with his closest friends; just get stuck in to the problem and get on with it.

Jan glanced at MacNeil, shrugged. The Chief knew what Matt was like. Then he turned his attention back to the glass wall, this time focussing not on the faint reflections in the glass, but on the subject in the other room.

This particular subject didn't look particularly naive. He sat calmly on the bunk on the wall opposite the glass, staring at the mirror. If he stood up, he looked as if he would be about six foot two or three, Jan's height. He had brown hair, cropped short, shorter than Jan's own hair. Brown eyes, unremarkable features, a largish nose. He might be about thirty—about Jan's age. He looked as if he hadn't shaved for a couple of days. *Do I really look like that?* thought Jan. He ran a hand over his own rough chin. The stubble was a nice touch; everyone around here knew

Jan hated shaving, while only the core Project team knew the reason, that he was actually getting into character, practicing with a steel razor literally copied from one in a museum.

The thought reminded him of the subject's clothes. At present, he was wearing a standard grey coverall, normal issue. But the report said he'd been picked up wearing a cotton shirt, with tight-fitting trousers made out of a heavy cotton material and matching jacket, and with leather boots. No synthetics at all. Definitely modern material, but all organic, and late seventeenth century style. It was, Jan decided, the weakest link in the story. Surely, anybody who knew as much about the Project as this guy knew wouldn't expect Jan to be walking around in period dress, fully in character, even within the Complex itself?

"Uh, Chief?"

MacNeil, who was standing at the window, hands behind his back, watching the subject, grunted.

"Have you thought that maybe this guy was actually hoping to *use* the Portal? Get in ahead of me?"

MacNeil turned. "Has someone been blabbing, laddie?"

Clearly, the shot had hit home. The Chief became more Scots under stress.

Jan spread his hands, in a 'who me?' gesture. "No, Chief. Just my finely tuned logical skills. It's what you pay me for, remember?"

MacNeil grunted again, turned back to the window. "And has no-one told you, then, that the Portal has been fully open for just two days?" It was Jan's turn to be surprised, but he said nothing. "Man-sized open, that is, not the pathetic mouse hole we've been playing with up til now. Open for just two days, with me thinking of sending you through maybe next week, and this character turns up, with some cock and bull story, trying to gain access. And if even you didn't know..." here, MacNeil turned, thrust his head forward at Jan, "...how did yon laddie in there know just when the time was ripe for his attempt, eh? And with you on leave, as well, so there'd be no chance of him bumping into you in the corridor. Eh?"

Jan decided to try to take the pressure off. "Unless he's telling the truth, Chief."

"Telling the truth! Here, scan his statement." He gestured at the terminal in the corner. "Check it all out, and then tell me if you think he's telling the truth. He's well informed, all right. Too bloody well informed. But he's not telling the truth. We've got twelve hours and more of debriefing there, all on computer, all transcribed and edited into simple English for you, laddie. Read it, have a good look at him, and then tell me who's telling the truth. I'll be back in an hour."

Jan watched the door close behind the retreating figure of his boss, looked through the window at his Doppelganger, who didn't seem to have moved. Below the window, to the right, away from the door, was the computer console and a chair. He sat, waved his hand in front of the sensor. The screen lit up with the word READY, soon replaced by the query VOICE OR SCREEN?

"Voice," he said. "First, I want some coffee, can you fix that?"

"Yes. On its way."

"OK, then I want the full story on that guy in the room next door. In his own words. My security clearance is . . ."

"No need for that, Dr Ricardo. I know who you are."

Oh yeah? thought Jan. *And if I changed places with that guy in there, would you still be so sure? Smartass bloody computers.* But he kept quiet. The smartass bloody computer was, he knew, smart enough to give him the intruder's story with all the repetition and questioning removed, as a continuous, easily digestible narrative. He could forgive it a lot for its ability at making information easy to assimilate.

The coffee was brought in by a security guard, of course. Probably nobody else was moving in the whole Complex except Security, and the Chief. He stood up when the door opened, nodded his thanks, took the pot over to the console, sat down again and poured a cup.

"OK. Begin."

"My name is Jan Ricardo, I work on the Gate Project, and I am making this statement under protest. I demand to see the Chief, Roger Jameson, and I hope that you are getting this message, Chief, because that's the only good reason I can think of for bothering with these idiots that are running loose in the Complex. As far as I can tell, the Project failed. Not the Gate; that worked perfectly, just as advertised. But from some of the gossip I overheard before they stuck me in this cell, things are as bad as ever outside, so it was all a waste of time.

"OK, from the top, then, though I don't see why you want all this common knowledge background. The year is 1968—one thousand, nine hundred and sixty-eight years after the birth of Our Lord, Jesus Christ, if you really want every detail spelled out for you. I guess we can agree on who Jesus Christ was, OK?

"Well, anyway, this is the ninth year of the Project. D'you want me to go over all the environmental stuff? OK. Motivation for the Project is to reverse the present rapid global warming. Every schoolkid knows how the industrial revolution of the seventeenth and eighteenth centuries pumped carbon dioxide and other greenhouse gases into the atmosphere, leading to the eco-catastrophe of the late eighteenth century. Things seemed to be coming under control in the middle of the nineteenth century, and by the beginning of the present century farmland was spreading south across Europe and over in New England. Then, about fifty years ago, carbon dioxide started increasing in the atmosphere again, at first slowly, now more rapidly. The reason is supposed to be classified, but if I can't tell *you* about it then the term 'classified' has gained a whole new layer of meaning in my brief absence.

"The problem is what those gung-ho technologists of the late eighteenth century, bless them, called a 'technofix'. Seems they decided that the best way to get rid of all the excess carbon dioxide was to liquefy it and dump it into the deep oceans, a couple of kilometres below the surface. Since carbon dioxide is denser than water, when it's liquid, the stuff was supposed to sink down to the bottom of the sea and stay there until the deep ocean circulation brought it back to the surface in a few thousand years' time. They reckoned that by then people would have sufficiently superior technology to be able to find a permanent solution. Pun intended, Chief; just to show I haven't lost my sense of humour.

"Crazy. But remember, this chain of so-called logic was brought to you by the same people who thought it would be a really neat idea to store plutonium in underground concrete bunkers, naively expecting that nothing would happen to it for ten thousand years. Try telling that to the people who used to live in north Wales. Oh yes, don't forget the ozone layer. Or rather, the lack of it. Another triumph of good old eighteenth century science. But not strictly relevant to my story, as the impatient pacing of my minder here seems to indicate.

"OK, back to the great globs of carbon dioxide floating about in the deep ocean. It seems they don't stay down there for thousands of years.

More like two or three hundred years, max. They're coming back up and getting into the air as a gas again. What's more, on the way they do nasty things to life in the upper layers of the sea. Not just fish; plankton, too, according to the studies carried out off New England last year. And we all know, don't we, the most important role plankton play in the ecosystem? Right. Fixing carbon dioxide out of the air and dumping it on the sea floor in the form of chalky shells."

"Pause." Jan sat for a moment, in silence. His opposite number was standing, now, examining his own image in the mirror. He seemed to be looking straight into the observation room, but Jan knew that was impossible. A cool bastard, though.

He was shocked by what he had just heard. The stuff about the carbon dioxide coming out of the oceans was highly restricted, and it had sent a shiver of excited surprise down his back as he had heard this stranger who looked—and sounded—like him calmly explain the details. Whoever he was, he had *very* highly placed contacts. But nobody had ever mentioned to Jan the threat to plankton in the upper ocean. It had brought him up short. It meant, one, that there were layers to this Project that even he wasn't privy to. Not really so surprising. But it also meant, two, that this imposter actually knew *more* about the project than the real Jan Ricardo.

He didn't for one moment doubt the accuracy of what he had just heard. It made sense, and besides, he was convinced that so far at least, the Doppelganger had been speaking the truth, at least as he knew it. Jan watched his double as he gazed into the mirror and plucked a long hair from his right eyebrow, then wandered around the room before settling on the bunk, flat out, hands behind his head.

"OK. Continue."

"So here we are, in the second half of the twentieth century, facing a double hit. All the old carbon dioxide kindly stored up for us a couple of hundred years ago by our ancestors is coming back into play, and in the process our nice friendly plankton are being killed off. This is not, as they say, good news. We need a fix of our own. Which is where I came in, or tried to."

12

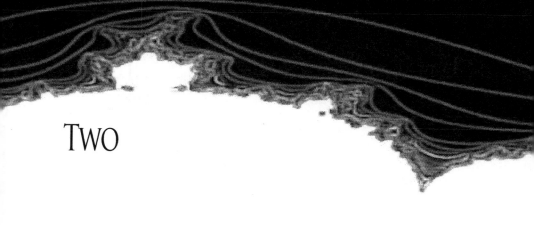

Two

I GUESS MY BACKGROUND IS PRETTY CONVENTIONAL. I WAS born in 1936, which makes me 32 next birthday (not until September, though). My family is Italian, which explains the name, but they settled in Scotland in the early 1800s, and I don't speak a word of the language, although of course I can get by in formal Latin if I have to. Useful when travelling far-flung corners of the Empire, or at academic meetings.

There've been plenty of those. I was always interested in science at school, how things work, and why; at one time I intended to read physics at University, but when the time came it seemed pretty pointless. You can find out how the Universe works, and what matter is made of, by reading it up for yourself in books. There's nothing really new to be discovered, and there hasn't been since Newton finally unified Galileo's theory of space and time with the Keplerian laws of uncertainty and probability. As far as fundamental discoveries are concerned, physics came to an end nearly three hundred years ago.

So I studied history, instead, concentrating on the history of science in the sixteenth and seventeenth centuries, when all those great discoveries were being made. And like everyone else in the fifties, I was increasingly concerned about the environmental threat hanging over our heads, as the warming set in with renewed vigour. Growing up under the shadow of global Armageddon tends to focus your mind on the past, rather than the future. I guess that's why I never really settled down, got married or anything. What's the point in raising a family in a world with no future?

Anyway, in 1957 I got permission to come south to Winchester to work for my PhD, at the very university where John Borodin had started the scientific revolution in the 1300s and Isaac Newton had completed it in the 1600s. I was 300 years too late, but I had full access to the archive (did I tell you I had graduated from Glasgow with 'special merit' and was regarded as something of a boy wonder in the trade?), and I was as happy as the proverbial pig.

Winchester is a small community these days, although it must have been something else a couple of hundred years ago, at the height of the Empire, controlling everything north of the Pyrenees and west of the Urals, and with New England still loyal. The University is an even smaller community, and there was no way that even a research student in history couldn't be aware of the odd goings on up at the Stones. I shared a house with, among other people, Matthew Evans, a research student in physics. We used to train together, keeping fit, doing some hill walking and climbing when Matt could be dragged away from his work. But that was less and less often as the investigation at the Stones developed.

When I did still see anything of Matt, he missed no opportunity to rub in the mistake I had made (his expression) in assuming the premature death of physics, however much his supervisor might have urged him to caution. He knew me well enough to know that I had really wanted to be a scientist, to follow in the footsteps of Newton and Halley. To have been born 300 years earlier, when there was still real science to do. So I learned, with an increasing sense of frustration which I worked off on solitary training runs, about his investigation of the forces associated with the circles that formed in the grassland on the plain each summer, and how tracking the field had led the team to a focus, a gravimagnetic generator of some kind, located deep beneath the stone circle itself.

At that time, late 1959 it must have been, nobody suspected that this was anything other than a natural phenomenon, although the Project was set up, initially with modest funding, to look deeper (literally) into what was going on under the stones. I was well into writing up my PhD research by 1960 (I told you I was good), and had time on my hands; the step from history into prehistory, with physics connections, was too tempting to resist. With Matt Evans, I wrote up a rather flashy, speculative paper linking the circle generator with the recurring circle motif in ancient England, the stone circles, temples, jewellery and so on. With some of the new dating technology, I found a marginally significant hint that the circle motif had recurred in ancient cultures particularly strongly at intervals of about three hundred years, from about 2000 BC to the present, and Matthew put in some numbers linking this cycle with cycles of solar activity, and changes in climate.

It didn't *quite* fit—the solar and climate cycles run at about 360 years, but we swept that under the carpet as best we could. I rather liked the idea that Newton himself, and Borodin before him, might have witnessed the same circle phenomenon, not in dry grassland but in the form of crop circles, in the glistening fields of wheat pictured in the Archive, on the very same Sarum Plain above the city where I lived and worked.

Of course, the climate connection has broken down now. It ought to be cold, a miniature Ice Age, like the seventeenth century, but the impact of human activities on nature has put paid to that.

Academically, the paper gave my golden boy image a bit of a dent—just *too* flashy and speculative. The one thing my peers seemed to approve of was the suggestion that the Stones themselves had been built on the site of the gravimagnetic anomaly in a response of the Ancient English to phenomena that they were more in tune with than industrialised people could ever be, except, as we were finding out, with the aid of artificial instruments. Somewhat to my surprise, the academic world rather disapproved, though, of my conclusion that since the Stones owed their existence to the anomaly, and were obviously a focus of prehistoric culture and religion, and Winchester had been built just about in the closest sensible place for a major city to the Stones—about a score of miles away, in the nearest large river valley—it followed that our very city, and perhaps even the great English civilization that had dominated Europe for almost a millennium, owed their origins to the anomaly. I guess that, even in this enlightened century, the Church doesn't like any hint that it might be descended from pagan religions. But it made a bit of a splash in the news media, and there was talk of doing a circles book. Then everything changed.

This was 1961. The Project had been running for the best part of two years. I had a PhD certificate with the ink still wet on the parchment, a short-term research job with the Cathedral, a flat, and Miranda. I was a few months short of my 25th birthday, and I was going nowhere, with no prospects other than becoming another dried up academic.

Matt Evans worked up at the Stones, and I saw him once a month or so, maybe more, just socially. They had been burrowing away up there, slowly but steadily, digging a little deeper each month and making more measurements of the gravimagnetic anomaly, occasionally publishing in the *Journal of Gravitational and General Research*, where it seemed to be an editorial rule that each page must contain a minimum of six tensor equations and be incomprehensible to anybody below the status of Professor of Gravitometrimagnetics. I lost track of exactly what they were doing up there, but I knew they were doing *something*, and it made me increasingly frustrated with my own dead-end choice of career. I guess that's one reason why the Miranda thing never really developed, though we got on well enough. We really just ended up as flatmates.

It was in August 1963, not long before my twenty-seventh birthday, that they sealed off the complex of tunnels up at the Stones. After that, when anybody mentioned them, you could always hear the capital 'C' hanging in the air as they spoke, and before too long it began to appear on printed records and in computer data as well—The Complex. We knew—everybody in the tight-knit academic community of Winchester knew—that they had found something up there. What, we couldn't imagine. Soon, I didn't have to.

They came on my birthday itself, September 7. Brought into my office by the Dean himself, who introduced them as Security (more capital letters!) and made it quite clear that I was to go along with anything they wanted. They gave me time to call Miranda, apologise for missing my own birthday dinner; then took me up to the Complex, where I met Roger Jameson for the first time. Of course, they—we—didn't have any fancy observation rooms then. Just a normal office, a little way underground, just off the main tunnel. 'Security' stood guard outside while Jameson introduced himself and explained that (surprise, surprise) his team had made a 'remarkable discovery', some five hundred metres down, dead centre below the stone circle. Then he sprang his joker on me.

"Dr Ricardo." (It was always "Dr Ricardo", then; I only graduated to "Rick" after two years on the Project.) "What do you know about the work of Edmund Halley?"

This, I may tell you, came as something of a surprise. But if there was one thing I knew about, it was sixteenth and seventeenth, even a little eighteenth, century science.

"He was a kind of maverick cosmologist. Lived around 250 years ago. Friend of Newton, but generally regarded as having been born a little too late. He was fascinated by spacetime geometry, but Galileo's theory had spelled all that out fifty years before Halley was born. So he dabbled in way out ideas, like the continuous universe theory. Probably ought to have been Royal Astronomer, but the establishment of the day thought he was just a bit too unconventional."

"What would you say was his wildest idea?"

"Well, there's plenty to choose from. My favourite was the discovery of the helium-carbon resonance. Beautiful."

Jameson's poker face encouraged me to go on.

"It's like the argument from design, only in reverse. Halley reasoned that the fact that we exist proves that complex atoms, carbon and the rest, are manufactured inside stars, since they must be made somewhere, or we *wouldn't* exist. Then he found that you can only make carbon inside a star if three helium kernels come together in just the right way, in what's called a resonance, to make an excited state of carbon.

"Mind you, there was some doubt at the time about whether it might be heresy. Mother Church was a bit less relaxed about scientific enquiry in those days. But in the end they relented, and Halley got his knighthood not long before he died."

Jameson shook his head. "No. I wasn't thinking of that one."

Suddenly, I knew. Without a shadow of a doubt. I *knew* what he was getting at. But the implications were too vast to comprehend. I played for time, trying to gather my thoughts, prepare for the next surprise.

"Well, there was that nonsense about time travel."

"Nonsense?" I'd never seen someone literally raise one eyebrow before. Interesting.

"Yes. Old Halley had a fascination with fantastic stories, you know. Used to write stories about alien civilizations. Well, he always claimed to have proved that there is nothing in the spacetime equations that forbids time travel. The Universe *allows* time travel, he said, but it is extremely difficult in practice, so nobody is ever likely to do it."

"Tell me, Dr Ricardo, how did Halley suggest that a suitably advanced civilization might set about building a time machine?"

"With black stars, of course. Collapsed entities. Put more than about three times the mass of our Sun in one place, and it punches a hole right through spacetime. Well, of course, there was no way anyone could hope to manipulate black stars, three centuries ago or today. But as far as I know nobody has ever been able to find a flaw with the theory. Matt Evans is the guy you ought to ask about that."

"Yes. I have." There was a pause. "You are aware, I believe, that this Project is investigating a region of unusual gravimagnetic field, underneath the Stone Circle?"

I nodded. It *couldn't* be. Could it?

"Dr Evans believes that it would be possible to make a tunnel through time—or space, for that matter—using something that even Halley didn't think of. He says that there may be very tiny holes in spacetime, far smaller than collapsed stars. Smaller than atomic kernels. The point is that *any* amount of matter will form such a hole, if it is squeezed hard enough. The Earth itself, if it were compressed to the size of a pea. A pea, if it were compressed suitably further. Anything at all. According to Evans, such microscopic wormholes, as he calls them, should have been created in the early stages of the Universe, the high-density fireball of the *Initial Explosion*. And if so, they should still be around today."

"Making it possible to manufacture a microscopic time machine?"

"You have, indeed, put your finger on the practical difficulty. With a pair of such holes, connected by a tunnel through spacetime, it is possible, according to Halley's development of Galileo's equations, to set up a kind of time tunnel. A very curious kind of tunnel, since it would enable you to travel in time only in steps of a certain size. A day, or a year, or three hundred years, perhaps. Enter one mouth of the wormhole, and you would emerge from the other mouth that long ago. Jump into the first mouth again, and you would hop back the same distance further into the past, and so on."

"If you were small enough."

"Yes. But Evans claims that there are theoretical arguments suggesting that it would be possible to expand a pre-existing wormhole. Perhaps even to man size."

"It's a neat idea. Has Matt published anything on it?"

"Not yet. It might cause too much excitement. You see, Dr Ricardo, we have every reason to think that the anomaly here is a local manifestation of just such a phenomenon."

"A working *time machine*? But even if the theory is correct, we don't have the technology. The technology couldn't exist for thousands of years . . ."

"Once again, you hit the nail on the head. It seems my advisers are correct about your talents. Yes. The suggestion is that we are at the spatial location of a time machine, constructed, for some unknown reason, several thousand years in our future."

By the time he actually said it, I was more or less prepared. But why was he telling *me* all this? Not just because I was friendly with Matt? Obviously not friendly enough—the bastard! Why hadn't he told me all this was going on? But there were more urgent questions to ask.

"How big, I mean, how far, well, can you use it?"

"The Gate is very small, about a tenth of an inch at present."

My disappointment must have showed.

"But there are reasons to believe that it will increase in size. You can discuss that with Dr Evans, if you join the Project. He believes that the Gate will get much larger, before shrinking back out of spatial existence in about 35 years from now. Then, it will return in about 300 years' time, from our perspective."

"Why 300?"

"We have had some success in using the Gate. Not forwards; that seems to be impossible, although we aren't sure whether that is a law of nature or simply part of the design. Maybe the manufacturers simply don't want visitors from their past. But we've been able to send imaging probes back in time. The pictures we've got—star positions in particular—correspond to the second half of the seventeenth century."

I thought for a moment. "And it may get big enough for a man to go through this, uh, Gate?"

"Yes."

Now I knew why they wanted me on board. They might, in due course, have a time tunnel big enough to take a man, leading back to the seventeenth century. The time of Newton, Halley, and the rest. The period of history that I specialised in. And they were all physicists on the Project, so naturally they'd want an historian who knew a little bit about physics. I blessed the moment of inspiration that had led to the publication of that crazy paper with Matt. *That crazy paper.* I sat up straighter in my chair.

"Three hundred years?"

He nodded.

"*Every* three hundred years, back into the past?"

He shrugged. "We don't know how far back, but several hops, all the same length, almost certainly."

"Tying in with the cycle motif? And the climate cycles?"

"We know that the Gate activity is linked with the recurrence of the circles in the fields, yes. It's hard to see how there could be a direct link with climate change, though. And I don't suppose even you and Dr Evans will claim that the Gate affects the Sun's activity." He laughed; I smiled politely. Let him have a justifiable dig at wild flights of fancy. If I wasn't completely mishearing what he was telling me, I was about to be asked to volunteer to go back in history and check out the scientific revolution of the seventeenth century.

It was like a childhood dream come true. No, it *was* a childhood dream come true! Wild horses wouldn't have stopped me from joining the Project team. Except—suppose I actually got to go through this wormhole, and didn't come back? The thought no more than flickered through my mind. I was in a job with no future, a relationship with no future, I was reasonably young and I kept myself fit. The seventeenth century wasn't the Dark Ages, after all; hell, I'd be better off there than in the present.

I was happy to sign (retina *and* thumb) anything they put in front of me, without bothering too much about the oaths involved in the Secrecy Act, or the fact that nobody would actually tell me exactly what I was volunteering to do until after I had signed up. Then, I found out just what I was letting myself in for. Jameson, and even Matt Evans, had been thinking along similar lines to the images that had flashed through my mind. As far as they were concerned, I was expendable. It would have made no difference if they had told me outright at the beginning; I still would have signed.

THREE

MATT GAVE ME THE FIVE GUINEA TOUR, ONCE I HAD BEEN signed up, assigned sleeping quarters, and issued with a grey coverall, my name already neatly embossed above the right breast pocket. Someone, clearly, had been in no doubt that I would be staying here, and I was assured that any belongings I felt I couldn't live without would be whisked over from Winchester by tomorrow. Miranda would have to take care of herself, for a while. I didn't even ask how long 'a while' might be, I was that excited. Besides, she'd effectively been taking care of herself for the past six months.

The corridor, sloping gently downward, started off smoothly lined, then became bare chalk for a short stretch, before ending in a metal door. Matt kept up a running commentary.

"We made the test borings very delicate; almost one molecule at a time. Came in on a spiral, you know? Checking out the field strength. But once we found this," he rapped on the metal, "we came straight in on the new tunnel. Been a bit busy since, so excuse the rough edges."

I looked more closely at the door. It had been cut from the slightly curving wall at the end of the tunnel, and fitted with a set of hinges and handles in a different material.

"Yeah," Matt continued, "it's a smooth, spherical shell around the chamber. We probed it with everything from acoustic to neutralino before choosing a place to cut the door. C'mon."

Behind the door, a short flight of steps, also clearly a recent addition, led down to the floor. We were in a segment, like a slice of pie, about twice man height, maybe twenty feet across where we stood by the door, narrowing down to some six feet across about forty feet ahead of us.

"There are twelve segments like this. Machinery, if you can call it that, above and below us," Matt gestured at the roof and floor, "and down there, in the inner chamber, what you've come to see."

At the narrow end of the wedge-shaped room, someone had painted a hand shape on the wall. Matt placed his own left hand over it, and a door opened seamlessly in the wall.

"Took an age to sort that out," he said conversationally. "Hit on it by luck. Young Faulkner hit on the idea of painting the hand on the wall."

We were now in a circular room, about twelve feet across and twelve feet high. In the middle, there was a rectangular frame, about eight feet high and four feet wide, made of thin, black tubing. On either side of the frame, at about shoulder height, there were two pads, mounted on slender pillars. The one to the right was a plain, matte black; the one to the left had a row of coloured lights along the top. To one side of this setup, a man and a woman, both in grey coveralls like Matt and myself, were sitting on the floor, engrossed in the contents of a small box. They looked up as we entered. The woman stood. Her manner was abstracted; clearly, we had come at an inconvenient moment.

"You'll have to excuse Jean-Pierre, Matt," she said. "This is proving a bit tricky."

"Don't worry. Ghislaine, this is Jan Ricardo. Jan, Ghislaine and Jean-Pierre. They're the ones who've unravelled this box of tricks."

She nodded; the man on the floor—Jean-Pierre—grunted. Matt steered me towards the frame.

"It's just a quick tour, team; ignore us."

Ghislaine knelt, picked up a small instrument, obviously more interested in her work than in visitors. I could understand that. I was itching to get involved, myself.

"Well, this is it." Matt spread his hands, did a slow pirouette. "What goes on upstairs and downstairs, I don't really know. Nobody does. We've looked, but we daren't touch anything. But this is the operating chamber, and it seems to have been designed to be more or less idiot proof. At least, we don't seem to have broken anything yet."

The room was lit by a soft, pink light, contrasting with the bright glare of the white lights in the pie segment outside. It took a moment to become accustomed to the gloom, to realise that that was, indeed, it. No view screens, no visible computer link, no consoles, not even a chair. A rectangular frame, stuck in the middle of a circular room, with two touch pads, at a guess, on either side of it. It was obvious what you were supposed to do. Touch one or other of the pads, maybe both, and walk through the frame.

Matt stepped over alongside it. "We didn't have a clue what it was, of course, so we stuck various things through to see what happened. Nothing at all, it turned out, unless you hit the pad first." He poked his own arm through the frame, demonstrating; wiggled his fingers to show they had come to no harm. "We left the left hand pad alone, at first. Too complicated. But when you touch the right hand pad, you get a build-up of field inside the frame. It's centred exactly in the centre of the frame, and, would you believe, it has exactly the same shape. A rectangular patch of gravimagnetic anomaly."

"But that's . . ."

"Impossible? Yeah, I know." He smiled. "Well, we built a little hoverprobe, like the one Ghislaine and Jean-Pierre have in that box over there, and we sent it through the field anomaly. It vanished, of course. So we built another one, with a homing beacon, and sent that through. Picked up the signal load and clear. Found the beast in the middle of the Stone Circle, with its little brother next to it. What we have here, we realised, is a working tunnel through space. A Gate from here to the stones up there. And it operates instantaneously."

"*Really* instantaneously?"

He nodded. "We checked. Of course, our communications with the surface can't go faster than the speed of light. But we sent signals at the time of departure, and we got a team on the surface to signal us as soon as it arrived, and we put a detector halfway. The detector received the departure and arrival signals at the same time."

"Which violates causality."

"Sure. Of course, we dug out everything on spacetime tunnels, going right back to Halley. And the bottom line is, just as you'd guess, you can't have a gate through space alone. Space and time are inextricable. Anything that operates as a space tunnel must operate as a time tunnel, as well. OK, you may be able to set the time dimension to be zero, to achieve pure spatial translation; but in that case you ought also to be able to set the spatial dimension to be zero, or very small, and achieve pure temporal translation. So we looked *very* carefully at the left hand pad, with its pretty coloured lights."

I moved over and took a look myself, taking care not to touch. "It's safe," Matt reassured me. "You can touch it if you like. Nothing happens unless you touch the other pad simultaneously."

The surface of the pad was the same matte black as the tubes of the frame itself, and the other pad. I rubbed my hand over it. The seven glowing patches of light along the top of the pad, a full spectrum from red to violet, were indistinguishable, in texture, from the material of the pad itself. Just radiant colour, instead of absorbent matte black.

"It's a number pad. Touch red with your left hand, the other pad with your right hand, and you get another field configuration. Same size, but when you send the probe through it comes straight out the other side. Touch orange and the right hand pad, and the same thing happens. Only, as well as coming straight out the other side of the Gate, the probe spends six months in the seventeenth century." He smiled.

"How do you know?"

"Fitted it up with full vid. It goes through the gate, out into the centre of the Stone Circle, sits there for six months, then comes back here. I mean, back to the same place *and the same time* that it left from. We set it to hover at 300 feet, photograph everything in sight. No doubt at all. Star patterns correspond to about 1660 or 1670, and we got some nice pictures of the natives. So we did it again. Got some nice pictures of the bug itself, hovering next to itself. Neat, huh?"

"Hold on. You sent it back *twice*, to the same place—the same time, I mean? And you got vid of itself, I mean the *same* bug, in the same place at the same time?"

He nodded. "The same four dimensional location. Location's the word you need."

"Where does the energy come from? I mean the mass energy. Galileo's law. If you duplicate the bug, you need the appropriate amount of energy to make the extra mass."

He shrugged. "I knew you'd spot it. We don't know. But that's one of the reasons why we're a bit reluctant to tamper with anything upstairs. There's another rig, up there. A sealed Gate, we think. It pulls in energy from somewhere. A *lot* of energy. Ample to make copies of hoverbugs—or even of people. And we don't want it being misdirected."

"People. Yes." I looked at the Gate again. It was still obvious. You touched the pads, and walked through. It *had* to be a human-oriented setup, not intended for tiny hoverbugs.

"There are indications that the field is changing. I'm sure the anomaly is going to get bigger. I guess it will fill the frame. But I don't know when, or for how long. When it does, we want to be ready. We want you to be ready."

I didn't want to think about it, yet. Needed to persuade myself that they knew what they were doing.

I turned back to the pad. "What about the other colours?"

"Yellow sends the bug back twice as far. Fourteenth century. Green another three hundred years, to the twelfth. When you get to the end of the sequence, you use combinations. Straightforward base-seven, with red as zero. Orange plus red is seven steps, orange-orange is eight, orange-yellow nine, and so on. All multiples of three hundred years, give or take a couple of decades."

"How far back have you gone?"

"Twenty steps. Yellow-violet. Six thousand years."

"Why stop there?"

"There's a snag. If you go back three hundred years, you stay for six months. Six hundred years, three months. And so on. The length of the stay halves every time you go one step further. At step twenty, we were down to 30 seconds, with the pattern still holding. You can't learn much about the world in thirty seconds. So it was a neat place to draw the line."

I tried to work the arithmetic out in my head. Dividing by two each additional step was easy enough. Two to the power ten, even I knew, was 1,024. So going back ten steps meant dividing the length of the stay by a little over a thousand. Go back twenty steps, and you reduced the stay by more than a factor of a million. So it would be 30 *milliseconds* at step 30, nine thousand years in the past, and three hundred *microseconds* at step 40, twelve thousand years ago. A law of rapidly diminishing returns.

Matt broke in to my mental gymnastics. "I'll save you the agony, Jan. It gets down to the Cavendish time at a little over fifty thousand years."

Cavendish, of course, was the late eighteenth century genius who had developed the subatomic theory of discrete states. Another of those key players, like Halley and Newton, who turn up at key moments in history. He'd shown that not only mass and energy, but space and time themselves came in a granular form, discontinuous. In his honour, the basic grains of length, time and mass, the smallest such entities that could exist, were given his name. The Cavendish time, I knew, was about 10^{-43} of a second—a decimal point followed by 42 zeroes and a 1. There could be no interval of time shorter than this, and that seemed to set a definite limit on the range of this Time Gate. No chance of going back to the time of the dinosaurs, for example, not even for a fleeting fraction of a second.

"I don't think you could ever go back that far, though, even in principle," said Matt. "You need some margin of error. Time to notice the Universe around you, and for the Universe to notice that you are there. Probably more reliable to set the practical limit at around the square root of the Cavendish time. That would give a total range of about thirty thousand years, maybe a bit less."

"But *why*? What's it *for*?"

He shrugged again. "Don't know. Don't want to know. After all, the only way we are likely to find out is if somebody, or some thing, steps out of that Gate over there."

I hadn't thought of that.

"But it's been abandoned."

"Has it? I hope so. We have to work on that assumption. But it still functions. We can't send anything forward in time, but I don't see any reason why somebody three hundred years ahead, or three thousand years ahead, couldn't send something back down to us. Believe me, there are people up top keeping *very* careful watch on the Circle."

There was a thoughtful silence, broken by the woman, Ghislaine.

"We're ready when you are, Matt."

She stood, watched her companion shift the box they had been so interested in round in front of the Gate. Inside the box, resting on what looked like a velvet pad, was what looked like a small yellow fly. No wonder they called them bugs.

Matt nodded to me. "OK. Maybe you'd like to do the honours, Jan. This is partly for your benefit, but we're also trying something new. Sending the bug back six hundred years, that's yellow on its own, but programmed to fly due south. It's solar powered, and in three months it should get a fair distance away. Want to find out if it still comes back, or if it has to be in the Circle for the Gate to grab it."

I looked at him, at the other two, at the Gate, back to Matt. I swallowed. "Now?"

"Sure. Stand in front of the Gate. Put a finger over the yellow light on the left, and your other hand on the right hand pad."

I did so. The space between the Gate's rectangular outline filled with a curtain of purple light, darkest at the centre, palest at the edges. There was a slight hum. The bug rose from its pad, hovered between me and the Gate at about chest height, orienting itself. Ghislaine, visible to one side of the Gate, checked a hand-held instrument, touched its pad. The bug flashed forward, into the dark centre of the purple curtain. Immediately, the curtain of light disappeared, and I was left standing at the empty Gate, looking at the bug, hovering in front of me at about chest height, *on the other side of the Gate*. Without fuss, it flew around the Gate and settled back in its box.

"That's it?"

"Yeah. Have to check it out, but it looks like I was right. If that thing behaved as programmed, the Gate pulled it back from somewhere over the Bay of Biscay, some time around 1360. Which means that if the anomaly ever does expand to man size, you can go through without worrying about how to get home. You'll have no choice. Anywhere on Earth, I bet, when your time's up you'll be back here, just like that." He snapped his fingers.

Ghislaine and Jean-Pierre were busy checking instruments, packing their box, obviously intending to take the bug away for a memory dump and view its records. But it scarcely seemed necessary. Those things always behaved as programmed, and if it had seen anything interesting, no doubt somebody would let me know. This Gate seemed pretty damned idiot proof, as Matt had claimed. Walk through it, and out into the Stone Circle above, three hundred or more years in the past. Go about your business, anywhere you liked, for six months, or three, or whatever you were allowed. And then, just like that, you would be back here, at the same time and place—the same *location*, I corrected myself—that you started out from. Simple. Magical—I remembered Fred Hoyle's famous remark. "Any sufficiently advanced technology is indistinguishable from magic."

Well, I couldn't even claim to be a scientist. I'd missed that boat, and now I had no hope of understanding the technology behind this particular piece of magic. But maybe I had lucked out, after all. For sure, there was no way that Jameson would let Matt go through this time gate, if that was what it was. Chief scientists were definitely *not* expendable, even if they might want to look at how things were three hundred years ago. And I didn't need to understand the tensor equations; what interested *me* was what you might be able to do—what I might be able to do, during the six months, or three months, in the past. There were distinct possibilities—*if* the Gate ever opened fully. They might think they were using me—Matt would use his own mother, let alone a friend, to find the solution to an interesting scientific puzzle—but as far as I was concerned, it was me that was using them. But was Jameson simply offering me a chance to do some historical field work? Or did he have some deeper plan?

FOUR

OVER THE FOLLOWING MONTHS I HAD PLENTY OF opportunity for historical research, studying the vid brought back from the 1660s by the bug. For some reason, Jameson and Matt Evans seemed reluctant to use the bug for repeated trips back to the same location, even though it *always* came back. Perhaps their reluctance had something to do with the occasion when it didn't exactly come back intact. Every single piece of the bug returned through the gate, but it had been crushed by a heavy weight—swatted, perhaps, in mistake for a real bug.

In itself, though, that apparent disaster led to a new understanding of the Gate. Bugs carrying little probes had already failed to bring back anything from the past, not even so much as a blade of grass. Matt now invoked what he called the Principle of Cosmic Censorship, postulating a law of nature that made it impossible to permanently mix up items from different locations. Just as nothing from our past could be brought forward in time for analysis, so everything sent back in time, down to the last molecule, must, he said, return to its original location at the end of its stay in the past. The scientific data and vid images in the bug's memory could come forward, he argued, because they only involved a *re-arrangement* of the molecules, or electrons, inside the bug. And in them same way, he hoped that a human time jumper would bring forward a full memory of what he had seen and done in the past. With admirable scientific detachment, but perhaps a little cold-bloodedly for someone I thought was a friend, he also pointed out that since the human volunteer would be carrying full recording equipment with him, a little amnesia on his return wouldn't matter too much.

In this way, there could be no lasting anachronisms—take back a palm computer, a beer cooler, or a helicopter (if you had a Gate big enough) and you might amaze the natives during your visit, but there would be nothing concrete left to prove that they hadn't been the victims of hallucination. Matt even suggested that certain puzzling stories in the Bible might be accounted for in this way, but Jameson quickly stepped on that speculation, refusing to allow Matt to put his ideas on record even in a secure computer file. The Project was already treading as close as it dared to the point where the Church might take an unwelcome interest in our activities.

The comforting thing about the Cosmic Censorship hypothesis was that it meant that when I *did* go back, I could take some modern aids with me—a Medkit, for example. Of course, I would be discreet. But even if there was an accident, and I got separated from my belongings (robbery was all too common back then, if the surviving records were a reliable guide, and the unspoken understanding was *even if I died back then*), when my time was up *everything* would come home with me, in however many bits and pieces and in whatever condition.

Although the team was reluctant to risk any more bugs checking out specific details, the material they already had on file was ample to sort out nuances of dress and speech that filled out the picture in the historical record. Back then, of course, they had only had flat screen film, mostly in black and white, relatively little of which had survived to be copied when the technology and storage capacity had improved in the eighteenth century. The voice material was equally sparse, although we did have a couple of recordings of Newton, from discs made towards the end of his life.

But by the summer after I had been invited to join the Project, I was as well informed about the science and times of the 1660s as I would ever be. I was ready to go, checked out on the colloquialisms and customs of the time, even fitted out with a good imitation of the appropriate clothing (remember, it was *cold* in the second half of the seventeenth century, the worst period of a little ice age that might well have become the real thing if it hadn't been for the greenhouse warming). Matt's anomaly had roughly quadrupled in size over those months, and at that rate I would be close to dying of old age before the Gate was open wide enough for me to get through. I needed something to do while waiting for Jameson to tell me just what it was he had in mind for my trip back into the past, and at last he relented, allowing me a full month away to visit friends in Glasgow.

TIMESWITCH

Miranda was no longer with me; she'd found the occasional weekend leave in Winchester, when my mind was in any case full of things I couldn't discuss with her, less than an enthralling prospect. I didn't blame her; our relationship had never been that big a deal, and as Jameson had reminded me, it probably helped to have no close ties if I was going to concentrate properly on the job in hand. So even in Glasgow, halfway through my leave I had done most of my visiting, had no one to show the sights to, and was kicking my heels, determined not to go back to Winchester, let alone the Complex, one hour before my leave expired—but still in need of stimulation. Which is how I came to be in the university library, scanning the copies of journals I had been failing to keep up to date with over the past year.

This wasn't entirely idle curiosity. Something had been niggling away at the back of my mind for weeks—maybe buzzing around my subconscious ever since I first joined the project. It just might be a big idea; but I knew better than to try to drag it out into the front of my brain. Better to let it simmer a while, and emerge when it was ready. It was so long since I'd had a really creative thought that waiting a little longer wouldn't hurt.

The break in Glasgow had allowed plenty of simmering time, and various half-baked possibilities were emerging. They all circulated, like moths fluttering round a light, around that old idea of a link between climate and solar variability. But I still couldn't quite put my finger on what my subconscious was trying to tell me.

So, naturally, one of the first things I did was to ask the computer for copies of anything that had been published over the past year that referred to any of my papers. There were only four citations, but at least one of them was from a paper in the weekly *Natural Science*, the world's most widely read scientific journal, founded by Robert Hooke and coming up to its tercentenary. I picked up the printout, and settled down to read it, with the aid of a cup of coffee.

The title gave little away—at least, not to me. 'Decline in the observed counting rate of solar neutralinos'. Neutralinos I had heard of, but vaguely. They were particles with no charge (hence neutral) and zero mass (hence the diminutive) that were needed to explain some of the reactions that took place in the kernels of atoms. Since the Sun was kept hot by kernel reactions, it was pretty obvious that neutralinos must be produced in the heart of the Sun.

31

I put the printout down, and turned back to the computer. It was a keyboard-only input terminal—I guess they didn't want too much chatter in the library—but it had full online access. A few keystrokes brought up some information from the database.

There was an observatory, deep in an old tunnel under the Alps, that specialised in monitoring solar neutralinos. Researchers were interested in them because, once they were produced in the heart of the Sun, they passed right through its outer layers and out across space, as if the Sun itself were totally transparent.

So the neutralinos, travelling at the speed of light (as any massless particle must) reached the Earth just under eight and a half minutes after they left the heart of the Sun.

This was interesting. I leaned back from the terminal and considered. One of the moths fluttering around my candle flame had just turned into a butterfly. I knew from my work with Matt on correlations between the Sun and the weather that radiant energy produced in the heart of the Sun actually takes millions of years to work its way out to the surface, before speeding through empty space from the *surface* of the Sun to Earth in that same eight and a half minutes (give or take a second or two). Which meant that the temperature at the *surface* of the Sun today is a result of some kind of average of all the kernel reactions that have taken place in the past few million years, and which meant, according to all the astronomers who'd come down on our paper like a ton of bricks, that the Sun's output couldn't possibly fluctuate significantly with a rhythm merely 300 years long.

My subconscious was screaming at me that all this meant something, but I still hadn't quite made the connection when I turned back to the sheaf of printout.

It seemed that there were fewer of these solar neutralinos reaching the Earth now than there used to be. The present experiment had been running for 87 years, apparently, with only small gaps for maintenance and so on. And there were other experiments giving a more or less continuous record back to 1774. In all that time, the flux of neutralinos from the heart of the Sun had been in line, allowing for observational error, with the way theory said the Sun ought to work. But at the end of the 1950s, the flux had dipped, and stayed dipped.

The simplest explanation of such a dip, assuming that the laws of stellar structure and of kernel physics hadn't changed overnight, would be if the temperature of the Sun's core had decreased by about 10 per cent, reducing the rate of kernel reactions and the output of energy from the heart of the Sun by the same amount.

As long as this was just a temporary fluctuation, and the energy output soon went back to normal, this minor hiccup in the core would never show up in the behaviour of the radiation escaping from the surface of the Sun, and fluctuations in energy output of plus or minus 10 per cent, on timescales of a few decades, would be neither here nor there in the billions of years lifetime of the Sun.

Only, there was an intriguing coincidence, which the team mentioned in a throwaway at the end of their paper, almost tongue in cheek. They referred to a pioneering solar neutralino detector set up down a coal mine in Yorkshire in the 1680s. The detector had never observed any solar neutralinos, which is why this field of research had been abandoned for nearly a hundred years. But, said the *Natural Sciences* paper, "it has not escaped our notice that a similar 10 per cent reduction in the rate of energy production in the solar core during the second half of the seventeenth century would have reduced the flux of solar neutralinos below the detection threshold of this primitive apparatus. One might even speculate that the 300 year periodicity in both climate and solar output claimed by some researchers (Evans and Ricardo, 1960) could be explained by a cyclic variation in solar core activity—*if* there were any way to transmit information about core energy output directly to the surface layers of the Sun".

So that was the extent of my precious citation. A cheap gibe poking fun at amateurs who didn't realise that nothing except neutralinos could travel directly from the core of the Sun to its surface in anything less than a few million years.

But maybe I wasn't so stupid. Another moth was turning itself into a butterfly. They were talking about one hell of a lot of energy. I always remembered just how much pure mass the Sun converted into pure energy each second, ever since my father had expressed it in unforgettable terms in response to my incessant questioning about the nature of the Universe, when I was about nine years old. The equivalent of one million elephants, he had said, turned into pure energy every second of every day of every year for nearly five billion years, and the Sun was still less than half way through its life.

A million elephants a second. It certainly put Matt's pathetic 'duplication' of a fly-sized bug into a different kind of perspective. Even the 10 per cent of solar output that seemed to have gone astray lately would be enough to create 100,000 elephants *out of* pure energy, if you knew how.

Or if you had the right kind of machine.

And a Gate capable of achieving a pure spatial translation, tapping in to the heart of the Sun from, say, a location in the chalk underneath a Stone Circle on the Sarum Plain.

Any sufficiently advanced technology is indistinguishable from magic.

So, what was the point of staying in Glasgow?

Within twelve hours, I was back at the Complex.

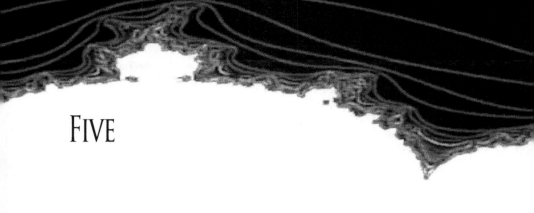

FIVE

MATT'S OFFICE WAS STREWN WITH BITS OF PAPER. HARD-copy from the computer printer, sheaves with his distinctive scrawl marching across the page in at least three different directions, actual printed and bound copies of old journals. Everything was supposed to be available in computer memory, these days; but somehow nobody ever had been able to dispense with paper. Especially not a theoretical physicist, a member of a breed that seemed unable to think without a writing implement to suck on and piles of paper to scribble on. In addition, there was the statutory blackboard, covered in equations in four different colours, with a big circle around the hieroglyphs in the bottom right hand corner, and the words DO NOT ERASE! printed in large red letters alongside it.

I was sure—almost sure—that anything really important would have been vid-transferred into the computer anyway. But if it said DO NOT ERASE! you could be sure neither I nor anyone else in the Complex would take an eraser to it.

What with all the paper, the small office was pretty crowded even with just the three of us—myself, Matt and Ghislaine—there. He gathered a heap of the stuff together, roughly squared off the edges, and moved it off the desk and onto one of the few clear regions of floor.

"It's a great idea, Jan. But how are you going to test it? Send back a bug rigged out as a neutralino detector to find out what was really going on inside the Sun three hundred years ago?"

"No need. If the detector they've got down in Switzerland is as good as they say it is, all you've got to do is ask them for their raw data, covering, say, the past year or so. Put a request on the link now, and it'll be back by return. After all, they did cite our paper; it'd be natural for us to be curious."

"And what will that show?"

"I'm sure you and Ghislaine have pretty good records of all your activity involving the Gate. Precise timings, in particular. Not much point trying to find out if the transfer is instantaneous if you aren't timing it in the first place."

"And?"

"I'm making a prediction, Matt. If the beast is drawing its energy from the solar core, and does so every three hundred years while the Gate is open, that would explain the overall suppression of the neutralino flux now and, assuming the old experiment was right, back in the 1680s. But what I'm betting is that when you actually *use* the gate, especially for time hopping, you draw even more solar energy. There ought to be little blips in the data record . . . "

"Corresponding to the times when we use the beast! Of course."

"Not to the *exact* times, Matt. If using the Gate draws energy from the solar core, it does so simultaneously, through that sealed unit on the top deck. But the neutralinos travel at the speed of light. The dip should follow just under eight and a half minutes later."

"That's neat." Ghislaine spoke for the first time. "I'll get on to it, if that's OK with you, Matt?"

He nodded. She turned to the computer console, began tapping at the keyboard. A request to the solar neutralino research centre in the names of Matt Evans and Jan Ricardo, thanking them for acknowledging our paper and asking for a downline dump of their raw data for the past year.

"But even if you're right, Jan, that doesn't explain the climate connection."

I shrugged. "I'm not really bothered. If we've found the energy source for the Gate, it explains how you can duplicate the bug by sending it back more than once to the same location."

"A hundred thousand elephants, every second. Yeah, there's plenty of leeway in the system, if you're right. But dammit, Jan, you're the one who persuaded me that the climate cycles are real."

"So, you tell me how the neutralinos can disturb the outer layers of the Sun on their way to us, and we'll have everything wrapped up in one neat package."

Ghislaine attracted my attention. "Got it." She tapped at the keys again, transferring the data into some number crunching routine or other. The big screen above the console lit up, with what looked like a scatter diagram, points dotted at random around a horizontal blue line. There was a helluva lot of noise there.

"I'm asking it for significant deviations downward, anything that might occur by chance less than five per cent of the time."

A series of vertical red bars appeared on the screen, highlighting regions where the scattered dots did, indeed, seem to fall more below the blue line than above it. It still wasn't very impressive.

"OK, now hold that while I call up my log."

The main display froze while she poked at the keys again. "Here we go. All the occasions in the past year when we used the Gate for time hopping."

A series of vertical green lines appeared on the main display. There was a clear correlation. There were some red lines—dips in the neutralino flux—where there were no green lines. But everywhere there was a green line, just to the right of it there was a red line.

My mouth felt dry. I had to swallow before I could speak. "What's the separation, Ghislaine?"

She tapped the keys, looked at the small console display.

"To the centre of each dip, averaging over the entire run, eight minutes, twenty seven seconds."

"Right on the nose! Hey, Matt—right on the nose!"

He seemed unduly calm about the whole thing, shuffling papers, sorting through the contents of a bookshelf. "Well, of course. It was a good theory. Bound to be right. Just had to teach the experimenters what questions to ask of the data.

"Ah. This is it."

He took down a volume, wiped dust from it with his right hand. "Knew I had it here somewhere. If my memory serves me right, we'll be able to give Ghislaine some real experimental work to do, and without scratching our brains too much, since all the hard work has already been done for us by good old James Clerk Maxwell, in—" he had the book open, and was running a finger down the table of contents, "—1870."

He could be *damned* infuriating. This was typical. Spend hours trying to persuade him you were right, then suddenly the locked door you were bashing away at swung open, while Matt gave every impression of having dreamed the whole thing up himself in the first place. Probably thought he had, too. But there was no point bitching about it; anyone who worked with Matt knew that. It was the price you had to pay for his singleminded, terrier-like attachment to a problem once he *had* got his teeth into it. And, clearly, he'd found something relevant in Maxwell's work.

"*What* did he do in 1870, Matt?"

"Answered your question, of course. The one about how solar neutralinos interact with the surface layers of the Sun on their way out. Only, nobody believed him at the time."

He passed me the open book. Keeping my finger in to mark the place, I closed it sufficiently to read the title: *Maxwell on Magnetics: Collected papers, volume IV*. He was a good bit after the period I specialised in, but, of course, I'd heard of Maxwell, a nineteenth century polymath who had worked on tight beam communications systems, and developed an enhanced understanding of magnetic confinement systems that had improved the efficiency of kernel fusion engines. It seemed he had also dabbled in gravimagnetics. I opened the book again at the page Matt had indicated; Ghislaine, abandoning the console, stood behind me, reading over my shoulder. "On the interaction between solar neutralino particles with positive magnetic moment and the solar magnetic field. Essay Awarded First Prize, 1870, in the annual competition organised by the—move your thumb, Jan—by the Gravimagnetic Research Foundation, New Bristol, New Somerset."

"Magnetic moments of neutralinos? I thought the whole point about neutralinos was that they had no charge, or magnetic field, or mass. Just gyre."

I looked at Matt. If Maxwell had won a prize writing about neutralino magnetic moments, it couldn't be completely crazy, but Ghislaine didn't seem any more impressed than I was.

He shook his head. "No *external* magnetism, Matt. But that doesn't stop it having an internal dipole."

I realised, dimly, what he was getting at—the important feature of a sub-microscopic dipole. Its magnetic field would be entirely self-contained, like a miniature bar magnet with north and south poles joined by a tight web of magnetic field lines, but no detectable external field once you were a few hundred radii away from the particle. And since neutralinos had an effective size down around the Cavendish radius, there'd be no hope of measuring their dipole moments directly. Equally, though, why bother postulating that they had magnetic moments if you could never detect them? My confusion must have been obvious; Matt began to get impatient.

"Not convinced?" He turned to the blackboard, wiped an eraser over the top two thirds or so, started drawing. "Look, the solar magnetic field is strongest just below the surface, right? Here. Where it gets wound up by the rotation of the Sun. Practically zero field in the centre, we know from the stiffness parameter, from mode 2 acoustic vibrations. So if there's going to be any magnetic interaction it has to be right here," he scrawled an X across the diagram, "where the field is not only strong, but transverse. You try crossing a magnetic field at right angles, carrying a magnetic dipole, at the speed of light."

Light dawned. It would be like trying to run through a dense forest, while carrying a long spear *horizontally* across your chest. *If* Maxwell was right.

"But what evidence is there that neutralinos carry dipolar magnetism?"

"Well, none at all, actually. It was Maxwell's conjecture. Suggested that energy dumped into the field by passing neutralinos was responsible for the magnetic turbulence associated with sunspot activity. Well, everybody and his dog has a theory about sunspot activity, and there was no way to test it, so it got buried. I came across it when we were doing that circles paper, but it didn't seem relevant, so I didn't bother you with it."

"There is a way to test it, though," Ghislaine said thoughtfully. "Basically, you need a very strong localised field. Obviously much stronger than the solar field, if you want to get a detectable effect in a reasonable volume. Beyond the technology of the 1870s."

"But not beyond *our* technology?" I was beginning to see what Matt was driving at. Dumping energy into the magnetic field could trigger disturbances, all right. And turbulent convection would bring up heat from deeper within the Sun, warming the surface layers and increasing the radiant output. I knew from the climate cycle studies that a variation of just 1 per cent, overall, would be ample to explain the 300-year cooling rhythm. It was one of those figures I used to shock people with, pointing out that the warming effect now being produced by greenhouse gases was seven times bigger than this largest of all natural fluctuations of the past millennium, and rapidly getting stronger. And there was always the intriguing coincidence, never satisfactorily explained, that there had been hardly any dark spots on the surface of the Sun at all, with very low levels of magnetic turbulence, during the second half of the seventeenth century, when the mini Ice Age was at its height—and when, I had now learned, the solar neutralino flux may have been suppressed.

"Pity we can't use the Gate to drain off a bit more energy. We could reduce the neutralino flux, suppress convection in the outer layers and reduce the radiative flow sufficiently to counteract the global warming."

I meant it as a joke, but Ghislaine seemed to take it seriously. She had been poking away at the pad of her palm computer; now, she looked up. "There's a possibility. I've got some ideas about how we might tweak up an ultrastrong field. Jean-Pierre and I have been analysing the anomaly in the Gate. There's a lot we don't understand, even now. But it's much simpler if you can separate out the magnetic effect from the gravitational distortion of spacetime."

For once, it was Matt who injected a note of realism into the discussion. "I think, team, that that may be going a little too far over the top for Jameson to digest just yet. We might have trouble getting funding for a thousand-year project. But it might be worth building a test rig to see if the magnetic effect works. I'll put a proposal in to Jameson. Give us something to do while we are waiting for the Gate to open fully."

Six

I NEVER GOT TO FIND OUT THE OUTCOME OF GHISLAINE'S experiment, of course. She'd got this impressive rig, set up in the wedge, complete with her own rectangular gate, about half the dimensions of the real Gate, with the neutralino source on one side and the detector on the other. There was nothing simple or idiot proof, though, about the appearance of the tangle of control systems, monitoring devices, and God knows what else wired in to the set up. It worked—after a fashion. She was generating a magnetic anomaly (strictly magnetic, no funny gravitational or spacetime effects) in a rectangular region, inside the gate, about six inches by four. Since nobody before had ever been able to generate anything remotely like that, especially not with more or less sharp corners, she was clearly on to something. But as yet the field involved was too weak to affect the neutralino beam, assuming it was ever going to have any effect. She needed more power, and the last I heard she was trying to persuade Matt that Jean-Pierre really had identified a safe power feed among the mysteries of the upper deck of the beast, from which she could draw off her share of the hundred thousand elephants a second, without the Gate itself noticing.

That was the last I heard because, out of the blue, the anomaly inside the Gate suddenly expanded to fill the frame. There was no warning, and nothing flashy about the process. First, there was the half-inch wormhole; then, there was a full size anomaly, filling the Gate. None of Ghislaine's instruments recorded any passage of time in which the change took place; as far as they were concerned, it all happened in the blink of a Cavendish time interval.

That was yesterday, 1968 time. There was no point in delay. I was ready—had been for months—but Jameson wanted a final briefing, I had no objection to a good meal and a night's sleep while the equipment was given a final check, and Matt assured me that the Gate would stay open for years. He specified 30 years, but I'm not sure how well-founded that number was. It sounded suspiciously like 10 per cent of 300 years, the interval between Gate openings, and just the sort of flaky guess that a theoretical physicist would come up with. It might have been more in character, knowing the way Matt approached rule of thumb statistics, for him to guess the square root of 300, which would have given me only a little over 17 years to get myself organised; not that I had any real problem about getting back to the present location, of course, since however long I stayed in the past my passage through the Gate would be instantaneous, here and now. But any worries along those lines, however ill-founded, were soon pushed out of my mind by the final briefing, when Matt joined Jameson to give me the parting pep talk.

"Well, Rick, ready to go?" I'd never been quite sure why Jameson assumed that he could put me at ease by using the old nickname. Hardly anybody except old school friends still used it, and I had no doubt that he had plucked it from my file, which doubtless included a lot more intimate facts about me than what I had been called at school. My real friends called me Jan. But I'd never bothered to correct him. I preferred it to "Dr Ricardo", and it did me no harm.

"Ready as I'll ever be. Full of shots against every disease known to humankind. Checked out on language, which hasn't really changed much since radio was invented at the end of the seventeenth century, and there's always Latin to fall back on. Wired for sound and vision. When I get back you'll know everything there is to know about how global warming got started, and why."

"Yes." He looked at Matt. "Actually, we're hoping for a little more in the way of active participation."

"Come again?" Jameson's passion for secrecy was nothing new, but springing something on me less than eight hours before I was due to step through the Gate was going it a bit, even by his standards.

It was Matt who responded. "Remember I mentioned what happened when we sent the bug back to the same location twice?"

I nodded. "Sure. You got vid of the bug hovering alongside itself. That's what set me thinking about the energy input required."

"Yeah. But what do you think the vid from the *first* trip showed?"

"Well, I guess that showed the second copy of the bug, of course. Just as on the second trip the vid showed the first version of the bug. We need a new language to describe all this business."

"We need more than a new language, Jan. You're exactly half right. The *first* time we sent the bug back, the vid showed nothing except the countryside around the Stone Circle. The *second* time, the vid showed the first copy of the bug. And there was a third trial, one the Chief didn't want me to mention to anybody, until now."

I felt a cold chill down my back. "Don't tell me. The third vid showed both the two previous versions of the bug. But neither of *them* saw the third version."

"Yeah. Got it in one."

There was a short silence, broken by Jameson. "The point is, Rick, it seems that it is possible to change the past. The seventeenth century didn't contain a bug, until we sent one back. Then, it did. Reality was changed."

"In a pretty small way."

"Suppose the bug had been equipped with fast-acting poison and a means to inject it. Suppose it had flown off, to, say, Rome, and killed the Pope. That would be a pretty big change."

"And you want *me* to change reality? Who do you want me to kill?"

Matt leaned forward. "The point is, you're *going* to change reality, just by being there. We've been avoiding overlaps since the early days, but every six months I send the bug through again to keep a continuous coverage of the region inside the Circle. None of the copies of the bug hovering in the air above the Stones has recorded an image of you stepping out of the Gate and setting off down the road to Winchester. But the one that came back a week ago covers the *next* six months, at that location, and you're going through in a few hours' time. When you do go through, you'll be able to see them, or it, if you take a sufficiently powerful viewer. And if I send a second copy of the bug through just *after* you, it will record both you and the first copy of the bug. Whatever happens, in some way history will be changed. We hope you won't kill anybody. That might be a little too drastic."

A sidelong glance at Jameson suggested that the possibility had, however, been discussed. I wondered who they had had in mind. Surely not Newton? But he wasn't waiting to give me time to think through the implications for myself. "So all we want is for you to change history the right way. Nudge it in the right direction. Discourage the runaway industrial activity."

"Hold on." I was still trying to come to terms with this. "How can I possibly exert any significant influence? If I tell them I come from the 1960s, they'll lock me up. If I don't tell them, why should they listen at all?"

"There's two schools of thought, Jan." Matt ticked them off on his fingers. "One, temporal inertia. In a nutshell, that means you can do anything you like, up to and including murdering the Pope, and there'll be very little effect. The further into the future from the point at which you interfere, the less the effect will be—it'll get damped out. Or, two, temporal instability. Chaos. The butterfly effect—you know, that famous butterfly that is supposed to be able to flap its wings in New England and change the weather in Europe because the tiny original effect snowballs into a cascade transforming the weather patterns across the hemisphere.

"On that picture, the further into the future from the point at which you interfere, the bigger the effect will be—it gets amplified. I don't buy that, because if it were literally true then even the presence of our bug, or bugs, in the past should have changed things dramatically. It's most likely that the real world is somewhere in between the extremes. If you change the past, there will be some continuing influence on the future—on our present—but you'll need a big effort to produce a big change."

"Unless you choose to apply leverage at a key point in history."

"Yeah, well, OK Chief, there are *three* possibilities. I was saving that one, Jan. There's a minority school of thought which says that everything stays put, unless you pick a key moment in history, but if you do the right thing at the right location you can change everything that follows. Like having a lever balanced on a fulcrum in just the right way so that even a small child can move a heavy weight; like, I don't know, if you went back to the 11th century and assassinated Sancho the Great, so the negotiations with the Moors broke down. The balance of power between the north and the Moors was pretty even, then. If there'd been war, it could have gone either way, but the world certainly wouldn't have turned out the way we know it, after nine centuries of peaceful coexistence. But we're not even thinking of trying that approach."

"So how am I supposed to interfere?"

"With information. Don't just observe the top people, get to them. *Suggest* the possibility of runaway warming. I've prepared a couple of papers for you to submit to the journals, letters to send to the quality newspapers. Try to get some media coverage—it should be easy. Just by making a noise about the threat, you may help to build up a groundswell of interest. And it may only take a small influence back then to have a profound influence in delaying the build-up of warming gases."

"And, Rick, if you don't succeed it doesn't really matter, because we'll be able to try again. Try something else."

I didn't like the way Jameson said that. "Like what? Assassination? Who?"

"Let's wait and see what's necessary, Rick. The point is, for now it's pretty straightforward. You ought to be pleased. Instead of just being an observer, you get to play the part of a concerned seventeenth century scientist. Isn't that what you always wanted?"

I was right. That file *was* pretty detailed.

"Won't they think it a little odd, anybody with all this expertise popping up out of nowhere?"

"We've given you a nice background, letters of introduction and so on, as a visitor from New England. Don't forget, the colonies were still pretty primitive, then, without very sophisticated communications. So we've borrowed the identity of an obscure physicist who worked in Kiowa. If someone checks the journals, they'll find a modest but respectable list of publications in your assumed name; if they decide to check back with the University of Kiowa, by the time the confusion caused by you being in two places at once is sorted out, you'll be back here."

"And if they decide I was an imposter, after I get back?"

"You can't argue with physics. It won't matter who you are, or where, if this stuff gets a public airing. It'll make people start thinking about the problem, a generation earlier than they did in the history we remember. That generation—fifty years or so—could make all the difference."

It made a crazy sort of sense. And, as they said, it could do no harm. While it certainly appealed to all my youthful fantasies.

"What's the name of this backwoods physicist I'm supposed to impersonate?"

Jameson smiled, like a tiger. He knew he'd got me. "Greenspan. Dr Thaddeus Greenspan. And don't let anyone tell you that a colonial PhD has any less merit than one from Winchester itself."

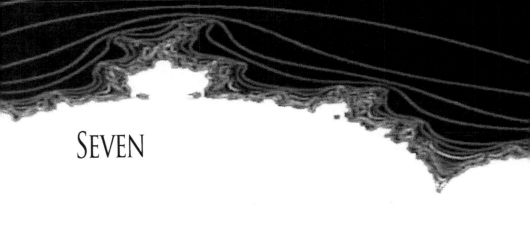

SEVEN

THE BIG SHOCK WAS THE COLD. BUNDLED UP IN MY THICK coat, I'd been sweating profusely while we waited for Jean-Pierre to finish checking out the monitoring equipment spread around the Gate. From their point of view, after all, I'd be reappearing instantly, and Matt wanted everything on record. Finally, Jean-Pierre nodded. There was no ceremony, no fanfare of trumpets or anything like that. Even Jameson wasn't there, at my request. The fewer the better, and everything on record so Jameson could view it at his leisure.

Matt simply said, "OK, Jan, when you're ready."

I mumbled, "I'm ready," and stepped up to the Gate. Left hand on the orange; right hand on the black pad. A curtain of purple fire in front of me. I stepped forward.

And suddenly it was cold. Bloody cold. I gasped, and the breath coming out of my mouth hung like steam in the air before me. I stumbled slightly on the rough grass, then stood still and looked around. It was morning, the Sun still over in the east. Good. We had no choice in the time when the Gate chose to disgorge me, although Matt suspected that there was a one-to-one correlation with the time sequence in 1968. Based on his tests with the hovering bug, he'd 'aimed' me at mid-morning, and it looked like he'd been spot on. Wait six hours, and I would have emerged in the middle of the afternoon; wait six months back home, and, assuming the Gate was still open then, I would have been able to step through and arrive here six months later. I looked up, waved for the benefit of the bug I was sure Matt would have sent through as soon as I was safely out of the way, and began trudging over the hard ground towards where I knew the road to

Sarum ran, just a few hundred yards away, concealed in a fold in the downs.

I hadn't been long on the road, walking downhill, stamping my feet hard to try to bring some life back to my toes, when I was overtaken by the land train. The noise of its approach had given me ample warning. The black smoke from its engine rose up over the sunken lane, and I stood well back at the side, watching with interest as it came trundling round the bend. The engine was clearly a coal fired steam locomotive, with large iron wheels supporting the cylindrical body. A tall smokestack at the front was trailing a modest streamer of smoke, the engine itself idling as the train rolled downhill largely under its own momentum. At the back of the loco-motive unit, a driver stood on a small platform, tending an array of brass wheels and large dials; there were no screens at the side of the platform to protect him from the brisk breeze that had sprung up, but a flat roof above his head, supported at its four corners by slender iron posts, gave some protection from rain or snow—and, I realised later, from embers thrown out of the chimney and falling back on him. Behind the driver, a boxed-in bunker stored the coal used to fire the engine, a shovel laid casually on the top. Behind the locomotive were two trailers, made of wood, with wooden, iron-tyred wheels. Each of the trailers was filled with sheep, pressed together so that they could not move. A farmer, on his way to market, perhaps.

As he caught sight of me, the driver wound a large wheel to his right, and the pace of the train slowed to little more than brisk walking speed. He leaned out as he approached, shouting.

"Are ye bound for Sarum?"

I nodded, shouted back above the noise of the machine. "Sarum. Yes."

"Jump aboard."

He clearly had no intention of stopping, but made room for me as I trotted alongside the driving platform, noted the position of the step, and then hopped up, more clumsily than I would have liked, banging my left knee on something hard. Once I was aboard, he wound the brake wheel back a turn or two anticlockwise, and the speed of the train increased. The warmth beating back from the engine, and from the closed door of what was obviously the firebox, started a tingling in my frozen fingers. It was obvious why this locomotive had open sides; the problem wouldn't be keeping warm in winter, but keeping cool in summer.

The clanking and hissing made proper conversation impossible, for which I was almost as grateful as for the ride itself. I needed a chance to assimilate the proper modes of behaviour without making myself conspicuous, even if I was supposed to be a visitor from across the Atlantic Ocean, who might well have literally outlandish ways. At least my clothing didn't seem to have struck my benefactor as odd.

"A cold mornin' fer walkin'," he bellowed, "and Saint Giles' day not a week gone."

"Cold indeed," I shouted back, mind as numbed by the calm comment as my feet had been a few moments before. St Giles' day was the first of September. This was barely autumn, not deep midwinter. My ingrained assumptions from the 1960s had already let me down; they would all have to be re-assessed here and now. Even in high summer, there would be no worries about how to keep cool during a mini Ice Age. For the first time, I properly appreciated, in my gut instead of in my head, that I really had made the time hop; and for the first time I really appreciated, with my fingers and toes instead of with my intellect, the difference between the mini Ice Age and our hothouse world. Good God, I thought. If this is the planet's natural climate, give me global warming any day.

EIGHT

I N SARUM, I THANKED THE DRIVER OF THE ROAD TRAIN AND
set about my first, vital, task. I had to have funds to cover my living and
travel expenses for the next six months, and a lot of thought had gone into
how best to set about this. Inevitably, anything I brought back with me
would disappear, as far as this world of three hundred years ago was concerned, when my time was up and I returned to 1968. However I financed
myself, there was no escaping the fact that it would involve cheating somebody—fraud, not to put too fine a point on it. We'd decided that the least
morally reprehensible thing to do would be to defraud one of the biggest
and most successful banks of the time. They could afford it, after all, and
the minor discrepancy in their year-end accounts that would result seemed
less likely to send ripples reverberating down through history than if I spent
forged bank notes lavishly among small traders who would all find themselves with unbalanced books at the end of my stay. So I had a letter of
introduction from the Bank of New Scotland, the most secure financial
house in the colonies; it was an impeccable forgery, copied from real ex-
amples of the time that were preserved in the English Museum, in London.
I also had, of course, similar letters from the University of Kiowa, introducing me to the academic world. And I had a weighty bag of gold coins,
still the most acceptable means of transferring funds in the seventeenth
century, that I was, like any traveller newly arrived from New England
would be, anxious to deposit with the bank of my choice in exchange for
some letters of credit, good at any branch of the major English banks across
England's European Empire, and some crisp notes to be going on with.

The gold, of course, was genuine. Jameson had been ridiculously pleased to obtain a loan of it for us, pointing out that at least this part of the Project wouldn't cost the government a penny. Personally, I thought he was simply showing his true colours, as a frustrated confidence trickster.

The letters of credit themselves also gave further proof, if I would need any, that I was indeed Dr Thaddeus Greenspan, a Gentleman from the colonies, visiting Winchester and London on scientific business. By one o'clock, I had not only completed my business at the bank but had used some of those crisp banknotes to good effect. Wrapped in a warm overcoat and provided with boots that actually did something to keep out the cold, even if they didn't look quite so good as the ones I had brought with me, I was ready to board the stagecoach that, I had discovered, left on the hour for Winchester. I had eaten well at breakfast, either six hours earlier or three hundred years later, depending on which way you looked at it, and rather than wait two hours for the next stage I was willing to leave my first taste of seventeenth century food until supper time.

The traffic was a curious mixture. In the narrow streets of the centre of Sarum itself, there was no room for road trains, but in the cleared area of land just outside the centre, where I had been dropped, I had seen three similar vehicles, two hauling agricultural loads, one with a burden of coal, being unloaded. Horses and horse-drawn vehicles of all kinds, from a pony trap to wagons and the stage itself, proliferated; but there was also the occasional steamer, relatively lightweight vehicles carrying up to four passengers, some with rubber tyres, burning some kind of oil. The internal combustion engine was being developed about now, over in the Hunnish part of the Empire. Within another generation, virtually all of the traffic in the major cities of Europe would be driven that way, and with the availability of lighter and more powerful engines the first successful flying machines would be being developed. If my stay weren't so restricted, I thought, I could make a fortune here, either as an inventor or simply by backing the right inventions, using the benefit of hindsight.

Outside the city, the traffic was chiefly horse-drawn, entirely agricultural, and the landscape developed into richer farmland, well wooded and with a profusion of hedgerows, as we moved down from the fringes of the plain. Only the occasional land-train provided any reminder that the industrialisation of Europe had begun. I had paid extra for a corner seat, with a view from the window; a newly purchased trunk, containing a few hastily chosen items of clothing and my old boots, rode on the rack at the back of the stage, ready to help establish my credentials as a travelling Gentleman. I was fascinated by the lushness of the countryside, an extraordinary contrast to the brown semi-desert that I had flown over so often travelling between Winchester and the Complex. But the swaying of the coach and the fact that, although I had not admitted it to either Matt or Jameson, I had scarcely slept at all the night before, soon combined to send me into a semi trance, half-asleep, half-aware of what was going on, but like a dream, as if I was viewing things through a reversed telescope.

I only came fully awake when we stopped in Winchester, and the doors on either side of the stage were both opened, allowing the icy early evening air to penetrate the warm fug that had been built up in the confined space by the combined body heat of eight passengers pressed in side by side.

As you'd expect of the administrative capital of the Empire, Winchester was an altogether bigger deal than Sarum, now as in my own time. There were more steamers in the street, but still plenty of horses, and flaring yellow gas lights, inefficiently adding their share of carbon dioxide to the atmosphere, along with a good deal of smoke, while providing a glow that seemed dim to my eyes, but was probably the wonder of the age for the natives. The inn sign creaking overhead carried the name 'King's Head', a picture of a generic, anonymous Saxon-looking king, and the date 'Anno Domini 950', which I took with a pinch of salt, although the place looked old enough, in all conscience. But it was too cold to stand and stare. I hurried into the inn with my fellow travellers, tipped the boy who carried in my trunk (over generously, judging by his reaction; I'd have to get these odd coins sorted out properly) and checked in. I suppose you could call it checking in. I must have looked the part, and the fact that I had arrived on the stage also indicated that I was a Gentleman, for the only thing the inn keeper was interested in was a night's payment in advance, giving me in return a key big enough to weigh down one side of my coat, had I been foolish enough to put it in a pocket, and sending another boy scurrying ahead of me to show the way.

"You can eat by the fireside, sir," he called after my retreating back, "or in your room, as it pleases you."

Food! The words suddenly made me realise just how hungry I was. "By the fire, please," I called back. "I'll be right down."

This time, I made the tip suitably modest. The boy looked disgusted, which I felt was the right reaction, but still knuckled his forehead in acknowledgement of the coin. He had lit the gas lamps in the room, and assured me that a maid would be along shortly to light the fire that was laid ready in the grate, a scuttle of coal handy nearby. The room certainly needed a fire, and I felt no inclination to take my coat off as I looked around. The bed was a four-poster, curtained to keep out draughts. I was beginning to appreciate that this would be an entirely practical idea, and owed nothing to the romance of yesteryear. The mattress, which I prodded gingerly, seemed to be stuffed with something that rustled. Horse hair, at a guess. The sheets looked clean enough—this was, after all, a main coaching inn in the capital of England—but it wouldn't be too surprising if I would be sharing it with an unwelcome guest or two. Well, I was full of anti-allergens and immunised against everything it was possible to be immunised against. I might get bitten, but I shouldn't develop any unpleasant rashes, or worse.

Over by the window, there was a china jug and deep wash basin on a wooden stand. I looked under the bed. Sure enough, there was a chamber pot. With any luck, I wouldn't have to use it. I'd make damn sure to visit the privy, presumably somewhere downstairs, hopefully not actually out in the yard, before I retired for the night.

The building was long and narrow, with its gable end onto the expensive street frontage. This meant that most of the rooms had windows, like mine, overlooking the narrow alleyway at the side, across which was the half-timbered, black and white side of a building, bearing the legend 'Goudbeyete House'.

Dinner by the fire seemed increasingly attractive. As I was leaving the room, the maid appeared, bellows, a bundle of long wooden matches, and some newspapers in her hand. Somehow, she managed to curtsey—actually curtsey!—without dropping anything, and mumbled something ending in "Sir". I nodded, held the door open for her, and said that I was going downstairs to dine. I carried the key with me, although there seemed little point. A child of ten with a screwdriver could have got into that room in thirty seconds, locked or not. Much more to the point, I carried in an inside pocket all my papers, including the money. If any child of ten cleaned out my trunk, I was rich enough to replace the contents once or twice a week for the next six months, and six months was all I had to worry about.

TIMESWITCH

Dinner really was one of those gargantuan efforts you read about in the history books. For simplicity, I ordered the special of the day, and a pint of beer. The special of the day turned out to be pea soup, with bacon in it, followed by a rather bony fish, most of which I left on the plate, roast pork with all the trimmings (including boiled *and* roast potatoes, cabbage, apple sauce and carrots), apple tart, and a large chunk of cheddar cheese, with bread and pickles. I gave up on the cheese after a desultory nibble, but managed to pack most of the rest away, along with another couple of pints of beer. Then, I could postpone the visit to the privy, every bit as horrible as I had imagined, no longer. Returning to the fireside, I ordered a pot of coffee and a glass of brandy to help me recover from the experience.

Around me, fellow guests and diners not staying at the inn were at least as busily employed as I had been in the serious business of eating. It was certainly the biggest meal I'd ever consumed in my life, yet it looked as if I might almost be the daintiest eater in the room, ladies included. I had, of course, had a long day, much of it out in the cold, some of it walking around. It was logical enough—you would need plenty of food energy, in this climate, simply to keep your body warm and your muscles working. Some of my companions were large—comfortably padded, as my mother would have put it—but there was none of the genuine obesity that you see at home. Manual work, as well as the cold, probably saw to that.

In spite of the similarities, the common language, the fact that these people were undoubtedly the same species as me, it felt more like being on an alien planet than merely being shifted three hundred years in time in my own home city. It might have been different if the inn had still stood in my own time, but I knew that right where I was sitting now there ought to be an open space, part of the inner city park created in the nineteenth century by clearance of the eighteenth century office blocks that had themselves replaced the older buildings in this quarter. A park that had only bloomed briefly, during the short period when the climate seemed to be coming under control, and which now—in my own time, that is—was as dry and dusty as the plains above the Complex.

It was all too complicated. I roused myself from my seat, picked up the coat that I had draped over the unoccupied chair opposite. The warmth, the food, the beer and the long day had combined to induce a not at all unpleasant feeling of drowsiness. Time for bed, in what ought by now to be a thoroughly heated room. Tomorrow, I would be presenting my scientific credentials at the University, requesting an appointment with Isaac Newton himself. And if there were any little companions waiting in the mattress, I doubted I would be sleeping lightly enough to be bothered.

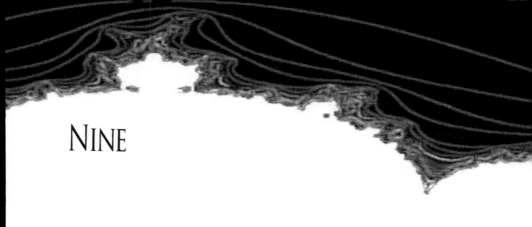

NINE

THE NEXT DAY WAS BRIGHT AND CRISP, WITH A LIGHT DUSTING of overnight snow. I made my way to Jesus College, which lay across an open expanse of grass from the old Cathedral of St Peter and St Paul, completed in the tenth century. The cathedral where St Swithun was buried, where Cnut had married, and where Harold had been proclaimed in 1070 after his rout of both the northern and southern invasions that had threatened his accession to the Kingdom of All England. It was a sobering thought that, even after travelling back three centuries from my own period, I was still twice as remote in time from the glorious days of Cnut and Harold as I was from my own twentieth century; it gave an awesome feel for the weight of years that lay upon the English rule over Europe.

But I wasn't here to study ancient history; my job was to try to change the present, for the benefit of the future. A small push, at the right moment in time; that was the theory. Like a lever, setting in motion a massive boulder that would, once moving, continue to roll under its own momentum. *If I could set it rolling at all.*

Or chaos. The butterfly effect. Change the world out of all recognition. But Matt said that was impossible; even the presence of the bug would have triggered instability, if instability was there to be triggered. No, all the evidence was that I would have my work cut out to make any kind of a change, pushing against the inertia of history. So I'd better get on with it.

I presented my credentials to the college authorities, explained that I was a scientist from the New World, travelling in Europe, that I wanted to meet Professor Newton. I expressed surprise that they had not received my letter, sent six months ago, to forewarn them of my visit (of course, there had been no such letter). A secretary, who seemed totally unsurprised by the inefficiency of the mail service from the New World, explained that Professor Newton spent much of his time at the new physics building, named after Galileo Galilei, the great physicist who had worked in Winchester a generation before. He was, of course, a very busy man; but if I cared to leave a copy of the paper I wished to discuss with him, there seemed to be some time when he might be free on Tuesday next, six days from now, in the afternoon. Perhaps I would care to call back then, to the College, to see if Professor Newton could receive me in his rooms?

I could have expected no more. Obviously, Newton would want to read the paper, which I was hoping he would pass on with his recommendation to the Royal Society, before committing himself to a private discussion with an unknown scientist from the colonies. I could only hope that he would grasp its importance and lend his authority to my relatively unknown name in ensuring that it was published. Everything was going as well as could be expected; but I still noticed that my hand was shaking slightly as I handed the precious papers over. Well, no doubt the secretary was used to that; Newton's reputation as a brilliant scientist was, after all, matched by his reputation for a violent temper, and an inability to suffer fools at all, let alone gladly.

But even if Newton decided that my paper, and my assumed persona, came into the category of foolish things, I had other strings to my bow. The paper was impeccable enough, and in the right style for the Royal Society. 'On the Retardation of Infrared Flux by the Carbonic Acid Constituent of Planetary Atmospheres', by Thaddeus M. Greenspan. It reported measurements of the absorption of infrared radiation by carbonic acid vapour (also known as the dioxide of carbon) in the atmosphere, and compared temperatures on Earth with those on the airless Moon and on Mars and Venus, predicting the possibility—*no, probability*—of global heating in the eighteenth century and beyond as a result of the industrial revolution. In what I thought was a rather nice touch, it speculated that great Ice Ages might be caused by a lowering of the carbon dioxide content of the air— something which would, I knew, be confirmed within a hundred years, by studies of bubbles trapped in ice cores from Greenland. I had another, shorter and snappier paper with me, to mail to the offices of the weekly journal *Natural Sciences*, reporting the results of experiments to measure the rise in temperature of the air inside various little boxes covered with lids of different kinds of transparent material and left out in the Sun. This rather neatly showed that a greenhouse made of glass actually traps heat by inhibiting convection, not by trapping infrared radiation, and made a cross reference to the Royal Society paper and to the way in which the atmosphere of the Earth traps heat. Then there were the letters to the newspapers, urging that the problems of pollution be taken seriously. But my best bet was to get Newton himself interested in the idea, and actively promoting it.

It was tempting to stay in Winchester, explore the old city, perhaps attend a few lectures and make myself known, in a modest way, to the scientific community there. But the risk of exposing myself as something other than a contemporary visitor from New England seemed too great. A carefully planned series of publications, and an equally carefully planned attempt to persuade the key scientific figure of the time of the importance of global heating, might just be carried off. But I dare not expose myself to the kind of gossipy conversation over coffee or sherry that would go hand in hand with attendance at any formal scientific gathering—where I might meet someone who, unlike Newton, actually had travelled in the New World and might know more about the University I claimed to hail from than I did myself.

But any regrets at tearing myself away from Winchester for a few days were initially eased by the fascination of the alternative—a visit to London, the commercial centre of the Empire. I travelled by steam-hauled train, the engine a monster with eight huge driving wheels. Another facet of the industrial revolution that was already transforming the face of England, and would in a few short centuries change the face of the world. But I was here, and I might as well enjoy it.

Enjoy it I did, travelling First Class and indulging in breakfast, lunch and tea, all served with spotless white linen, genuine china, and silver cutlery. It was just as well the experience was so delightful, since never can there have been a better example of it being better to travel hopefully than to arrive.

London itself was a great disappointment. Dirty, smelly and cramped, dominated by wooden houses crammed into narrow streets and lanes. The plumbing was a disaster, and the River Thames, the very reason for the city's existence as a commercial centre and trading port, was like an open sewer, stinking from the filth that poured into it untreated, and which slopped up and down river on every tide. This was London at its worst, almost twenty years before the great fire that would sweep through the tinder dry buildings during the Great Frost of 1683–84, adding the devastation of fire to the harshest winter of the millennium. It was easy to see why King, Court and Parliament had never been tempted to move from the cleaner environment of Winchester to the financial heart of the Empire.

After two days, I had had enough, and returned slowly back to the capital myself, by stage, stopping at a series of coaching inns along the way. On Monday night, I was back at the King's Head; on Tuesday, I presented myself, as anxious as a PhD student awaiting his oral examination, back at Jesus College.

TEN

THE SECRETARY RECOGNISED ME, AND SMILED A GREETING. Professor Newton was, he said, fascinated by my paper, and had expressed interest in communicating it, on my behalf, to the Royal Society. If I would care to follow the secretary, he would lead me to the Professor's rooms.

We crossed—or rather, walked around the edge of—a quiet quadrangle. Just as in my day, only Fellows of the College were allowed to walk on the grass, not that much grass was visible under the snow. On three sides, the quad was almost indistinguishable from its appearance in the twentieth century, except for the absence of electric light. On the fourth side, where the new Chapel ought to have been, there was simply a continuation of the windows and doorways set in the familiar stone walls of the other three sides. We entered a doorway in the corner of the quad, and mounted a flight of wooden steps, curving slightly and emerging on a landing in front of an oak door. The secretary knocked, opened the door without waiting for a reply, and ushered me in with the announcement "Dr Greenspan, sir."

The room was small, gaslit against the gloom of the overcast afternoon outside, lined with books and littered with papers. It reminded me, immediately, of Matt's chaotic nest back at the Project, except that Matt's office never had a glowing open fire in the wall opposite the desk. As I entered, the man behind that desk flung down some papers, pushed back his chair, and rose to his feet.

"Damn the man! Such effrontery!" He noticed my presence, and grunted. "Not you, not you. Pray, be seated."

As I moved towards the chair indicated, a comfortable arm chair at the fire side, matched by a companion opposite, Newton stalked away from the desk, and stood directly in front of the fire place, turning his back to the warmth of the flames. I stood by the chair, uncertain whether I should sit before he did. Perhaps I should have. I was completely wrong-footed by his next remark.

"So, why do you want to bother with the Royal, eh? Bunch of nincompoops. Damn fine piece of work, that paper you sent me. Too good for the likes of Hooke. Why bother with them, eh?"

The famous temper had clearly been roused. Hooke, obviously, was Robert Hooke, one of Newton's regular sparring partners, who had made—would make—some important contributions to the theory of radiation. It seemed best to find out how he had upset Newton, before pressing my own case.

"Surely, sir, the Royal Society is the best place to promulgate new ideas? I would welcome your advice, but in my part of the world, we regard the Royal as the seat of scientific authority."

"Maybe so. In the abstract, maybe. The idea of the Society is noble enough. But when they allow such small-minded, incompetent, so-called scientists . . . "

He trailed off, the anger dissipating slightly. But I was intrigued. The battles between Newton and Hooke were part of scientific and historical legend, and here I was, in the middle of one. Surely, it wouldn't do any harm to play the part of historian for a few minutes? I guessed that the row must be the one about Newton's corpuscular theory of light; the timing was about right, although I'd have to be careful how much knowledge I revealed, since nothing much would be published formally for another five years, thanks to Newton's notorious reluctance to go into print. Generalities seemed the best opening bet.

"Of course, sir, the Royal must provide a forum for debate. Freedom of speech, even for those of lesser ability, is enshrined in our Constitution. And then, it seems to me, that the greater intellect must always prevail, shining like a beacon of truth compared with the arguments of lesser men."

He turned sideways to the fire, looking at me carefully. I hoped he didn't doubt my sincerity. Obviously, he liked what he saw.

"Well enough. Freedom of speech, yes. And the right to enquire into the nature of the world, from Athelstan's time right down to the present day.

But *not*," here his voice rose again, "slanderous accusations. With freedom goes responsibility. No responsible scientist would steal the work of another man. The accusation is intolerable. And yet people take him seriously. Why? Why? Surely it cannot simply be out of pity for the little runt, with his twisted back and his limp?" The last words were almost spat out. I had to soothe him more.

"Sir, I cannot imagine that anyone doubts your word. Perhaps Hooke has simply misunderstood. Can you tell me about these new discoveries you have made? It takes so long for news to reach us in New England."

"Indeed." He looked around the room, then settled in the other easy chair, across the fireplace, gesturing again for me to occupy the seat I had been standing beside. "But you have not come here to discuss my corpuscular theory of light, Dr Greenspan. Your own work is intriguing, and of much greater practical relevance to the problems facing society today. The notion that the world cools when there is a lack of carbonic acid vapour in the atmosphere. Absolutely fascinating."

I scarcely took in his comments about my work, except to note that he was obviously sufficiently impressed to give it the recommendation I needed, once he had calmed down. It *was* the corpuscular theory! The mention of the basis of the row with Hooke really caught my attention. This was one of the key moments in scientific history! The culmination of seven hundred years of the Anglo Saxon tradition of enquiry and education.

And now Newton was taking the next step, establishing the corpuscular nature of light! The particle-wave duality! The repercussions would echo down the next three centuries. The implication, that Nature is discontinuous at the fundamental level, with waves behaving like particles and particles like waves. The inference that precise position, and precise time, had no meaning, that the Universe did not run along pre-ordained rails like some great clockwork engine, but contained inherent uncertainty and indeterminacy. And that if nothing was fixed and certain, then maybe there might, after all, be a means to transmute one element into another, using the energy which Galileo's famous equation, $E = mc^2$, said was locked up in the heart of every atom.

But how much of this could I be expected to know?

"Surely, the Cartesian equations of light have established that it is purely an electromagnetic wave?"

He smiled, and leaned forward in his chair. "If you *look* for a wave, Dr Greenspan, then you will find a wave. I refer to the double-slit experiments, the interference patterns and so on. An experiment designed to measure the wave nature of light, or of any other electromagnetic wave, will indeed measure wave properties. But it is my contention that an experiment designed to measure *particle* properties of light will always reveal its corpuscular nature. We have just such an experiment, over at the Galileo lab; but I won't bore you with the details. What matters is that wave and corpuscle are two facets of the character of light, like opposite sides of a coin. You can only ever measure one at a time, but both are equally real." He sat back, still with a satisfied smile.

"And Hooke doesn't believe this?"

The smile disappeared. "Believe it? Oh, he *believes* it, indeed. More than that. He claims to have thought of it first! Bah! Oh yes, he developed some of the Cartesian equations to take account of the statistical behaviour of radiators and absorbers. Indeed, he made a modest contribution to our understanding of the way atoms interact with radiation. *But he never suggested that light is composed of corpuscles.* I will *not* retract, no matter how much that fool Jones may plead. Infernal Welshman. What does he know?"

Everything fell into place. Jones, I knew from my studies, would have been Secretary of the Royal Society, the Society founded by Athelstan III, at this time. Hooke, learning of Newton's corpuscular theory, had claimed the idea had been stolen from him; Newton had called Hooke a liar. In the seventeenth century, this was serious stuff. Some people still fought duels over matters of honour, although the practice had been illegal since 1592. Somebody had to retract, or the row threatened to split the Royal in two. And Hooke was the older man, long established in the Royal Society, while Newton, in spite of his acknowledged genius, could still be considered a brash upstart. Jones, an establishment man to his core, wanted Newton to be the one to do the placating.

Because of the argument, Newton would sit on his idea for years, polishing it and refining it with the aid of more experiments, before publishing. But history also said that he had found a way to placate Hooke, and meet the demand from Jones for a formal apology, without losing too much face. Perhaps a little nudge would do no harm.

"Surely, sir, it is beneath your dignity to be disturbed by these accusations from Hooke. He is, you say, a small man; it seems to me he is small minded, too. Whereas you are renowned as a giant among scientists, in the line of other giants such as Borodin, Descartes, Galileo . . . "

"Giants. Yes, my work has indeed been built upon that of giants, not drawn from the scribblings of a pygmy like Hooke, a pygmy who only followed where Descartes led." Suddenly the smile was back on his face. "Come, Dr Greenspan, you have brought me inspiration." He stood and hurried to the desk, shoving papers to one side, pulling out a pen and beginning to write on a clean sheet. He muttered as he wrote.

"I shall reply to the esteemed Dr Hooke, in the sweetest possible tones. 'Placate Hooke', Jones says, and placate Hooke I will. What d'you think of this?" And he read out what he had written, explaining as he went along.

"*What Descartes did was a good step.* Well, no quarrel with that, surely; and for those with wit to see, a clear reminder that Descartes did his great work before Hooke came on the scene. Now, to make myself completely clear, *You have added much in several ways, and especially in taking the radiation of ideal absorbers into philosophical consideration.* What could be more pleasant? And what could say more clearly that Hooke merely refined Descartes' work? Now, I'll add a few flowery phrases here, some meaningless formality about the limitations of my own ability, purely a matter of form, everyone knows that is just a politeness. Then, I shall use your expression, with permission, Dr Greenspan. *If I have seen further it is by standing on the shoulders of giants.* And not, you understand, by plagiarising the work of dwarves. Hah!"

He rubbed his hands with glee. "Shall I put a capital letter on Giants, d'you think? Rub the point home, hmm? Yes, I think so." And he scribbled on the page again, then stood back to admire it. "Yes, indeed, this will fit the bill. Hooke will have to accept it as an apology; Jones will be content; and all those with eyes to see will read the true message.

"What time is it?" Without waiting for an answer, he pulled a watch from his pocket, studied it. "I must make a fair copy of this, have it delivered by hand to Hooke this very day, with a copy to Jones. Dr Greenspan, I regret that our discussion is at an end. But I am grateful to you, very grateful, for showing me how to deal with Hooke. And as for your paper, why, have no worries on that score. I will send it with this letter. Jones will be so pleased with my conciliatory tone towards Hooke, that he will have it read at the very next meeting of the Royal, and published in the *Proceedings.*"

Suddenly, things were moving too fast. We hadn't actually discussed global heating at all; I had had no opportunity to make my case. Would I get another opportunity? It seemed unlikely, from the way Newton was ushering me, politely but firmly, towards the door. And yet, I had achieved my main objective, after all. The paper would be noticed. For those with eyes to see, the message would indeed be plain.

I made my farewells, shook Newton by the hand (actually shook *Isaac Newton* by the hand!) and went on my way, slightly dazed. I had a clear choice. I could either stay in Winchester until my time was up, risking being uncovered as an imposter on the chance of finding another opportunity to discuss global heating with Newton, or I could travel north, as I had originally planned, carrying out my proper role of historian, gathering information to take back to the twentieth century. The choice was pretty straightforward. I had done everything Jameson and Matt had asked of me. If their scheme was going to work out, it would. If it didn't, then assuming Matt was right they had 30-odd years to dream up a better one, making full use of my historical survey, and send someone else back to carry it out, before the Gate closed. Damn it, I *am* an historian, and it made sense to plan properly before trying to change the past. I had my doubts about the whole scheme, anyway; I was beginning to hope that my actions *hadn't* changed reality, and I certainly wasn't going to act beyond the letter of my instructions, on my own initiative.

But maybe I should have. The story of my travels in the seventeenth century hardly seems important, now, in view of what I have come back to. *Did* I change the past? The Project is still here, as far as I can tell the global heating is as bad as ever, but there's no Jameson, no Matt, and I'm being treated like a spy. What the Hell is going on?

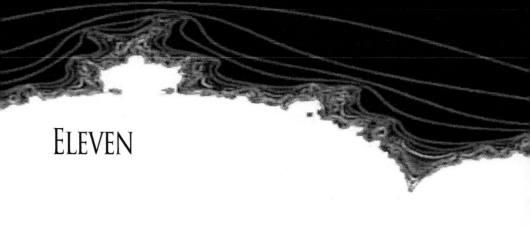

ELEVEN

JAN HAD BEEN LISTENING TO THE STORY WITH HIS EYES CLOSED, leaning back in the swivel chair. Now, he opened his eyes, swung the chair to face the observation window, studied his Doppelganger for a moment. The imposter was lying on his bed, eyes closed.

"Tell MacNeil I'm ready for him."

"He's already on his way, Dr Ricardo. With Dr Evans."

Trust MacNeil to have the briefing timed to the second. Or to have this room bugged, purely in the interests of efficiency. Of course, it was the right thing to do. But it still got Jan's back up. Just once, he'd like to see MacNeil fall flat on his face, make some kind of simple mistake, like other people did.

The door opened while the thought was still forming. MacNeil wasted no time on formalities; Matt merely nodded, mouthed a silent "Hi" over the chief's shoulder as he spoke.

"What do you make of him?"

"He's good. Very good. But there are some big holes in his story."

"Give me an example."

"Well, on the personal side, I do know a girl called Miranda, went out with her a couple of times. But it was never anything serious. Then there's the science side. Either he knows more than I do about this Project, or he's wrong about the effect of oceanic carbon dioxide release in plankton. I hope he's wrong." Jan stopped, looking expectantly at MacNeil. It was Matt, seemingly bubbling with barely suppressed excitement, who answered.

"We don't know anything about that either, Jan. It sounds plausible. I've asked some of the people in New England to look into it."

"But as of now, it is a complete fiction, Matt. That is the important point. And just the kind of plausible fiction anyone with inside knowledge of the Project could invent." MacNeil had clearly made up his mind about the imposter. Matt shrugged. Matt never made up his mind about anything until he had good evidence. Jan tried to get them back on track.

"But what about the equipment he claims to have been carrying? The letters of introduction? The gold? They should all have come back with him, if his story is true."

"That's the clincher. Of course, he isn't wired for sound and vision, and I'll bet he never was. He's got all the letters and papers he mentions, good forgeries on real paper with ink manufactured from vegetable dyes. But no non-organic artifacts of any kind. Not even the gold."

"Which could be due to some aspect of the Portal that we don't understand. Something connected with the way this guy has been wandering around in the 1660s. After all, according to his story it was the first time a living person had used the Portal, at least in our location."

"So why, Matt, do automated probes come back happily on their own but not if they are attached to a living person?"

"I don't know. We'd have to do some tests to find out."

"*If* this guy's story was real."

It was time for the shrug again. But the noncommittal gesture was belied by the sparkle in his eye. Matt, Jan could see, was prepared to accept the imposter's story as a working hypothesis, and test it, either to destruction or to the point where it was proved true. MacNeil saw no need for such tests. He *knew* the imposter was lying. Jan simply didn't know. Logic told him that the story couldn't possibly be true. But why, then, was the intruder in the Complex? What was he trying to achieve?

"You said the papers were good forgeries?"

"Perfect. Exactly accurate, of course, but that's easy. Anybody could look up the *Proceedings* of the Royal Society for February 1668 and copy out a paper by Thaddeus M. Greenspan. It's not as if it were even an obscure paper, really. Everyone on the Project knows that it was Greenspan's prescient ideas about the link between Ice Ages and a decline in the carbon dioxide content of the air that encouraged the pro-coal lobby to regard carbon dioxide pollution as the saviour of the world, preventing the cold of the seventeenth century developing into a full-blown Ice Age there and then. God knows, they might even have been right. That was one of the reasons why the anti-coal lobby never really stood a chance at the beginning of the eighteenth century."

"And yet this guy next door is claiming that the paper was a forgery, which he took back three hundred years and persuaded Newton to present to the Royal on his behalf?"

Matt made a circle with the middle finger and thumb of his right hand, held it up, looked at Jan through the ring. "Exactly. If he *did* change the past, he changed it the opposite way to which he intended. Shows the danger of meddling in things you don't understand."

"And he came *back* to a different future? Our present? One he'd never left from, which is why I'm still here, and he's here too?"

"Leverage, Jan. He had enough leverage to make a few small changes, nothing more. No butterfly effect. No chaos."

MacNeil interrupted. "This is complete nonsense. What we have to find out is what the intruder is doing here. For God's sake don't start taking his ridiculous cover story so seriously."

There was a short silence, broken by Jan. "Where do you come in, Chief? Why does he seem to think the Project is being run by somebody called Jameson?"

For the first time, MacNeil's assurance crumbled slightly.

"There was a Jameson, Alun Jameson. Worked in the Department. Two years my senior. Killed in a flying accident in 1959. If he'd lived, he might well have been in line for a job like this. Probably would've been better at it than I am." He regained his composure. "Certainly wouldn't have been slack enough to let an intruder get right through to the Portal without being spotted."

"So what do you want me to do?"

"Confront him. Face to face. His story won't stand up once he sees you are in the Complex, and he'll have to come up with something new, even if it's still not the truth. Whatever his next story is, it may give us a lead."

"I need some time to think about this."

"Don't take too long, Dr Ricardo. This *is* an emergency."

"Uh, Chief?" Matt's excitement was still just being kept in check. "Can I discuss this with Jan first? Alone? Help him to make up his mind?"

"If you insist. I'll leave you to it. But I want some action soon, and I don't want any more nonsense about accepting his story at face value."

MacNeil turned to go, but something was nagging at Jan's mind.

"One question, Chief." MacNeil stopped. "What about the assassination idea? Any truth in that?"

He didn't turn round. "There is an experimental weapon in the armoury. It fires a metal arrow, rather like a crossbow bolt. Uses magnetic induction. If somebody used such a device to commit a murder in 1668, and the weapon returned to this *location* after use, it might be the perfect crime. If anyone had any reason to carry out such a deed." He opened the door and was gone.

Matt whistled, softly. "The old boy must be rattled, Jan. He's never breathed a word of that to me. So he *is* thinking of changing the past. I wonder who he has in mind for a victim."

"It's obvious. Thaddeus M. Greenspan. The author of that greenhouse/Ice Age paper that made everyone think carbon dioxide was good for you. Why else would he have all that stuff off pat? *I'm* the historian, not him."

"No wonder he's so worried by your story."

"My story?"

Matt nodded at the observation window. "Let's face it, Jan, he *is* you. An alternative you. I guess MacNeil's got his own reasons for being unable to accept it—God knows what they are—but to me it's the simplest working hypothesis. Take it at face value until it's proved wrong. Why would he make up that Jameson business?"

"He could hardly claim to know MacNeil, could he? Pretending the Chief isn't the Chief would confuse us, make people like you more willing to believe him."

"So why does he claim to come from 1968? Why pretend he started his time journey from two years into our future? There's no possible motive for that. He claims the gate wasn't even open in 1966."

"Then why didn't he go back to 1968, if his story is real?"

"Good point. But put it together with the rest." Matt paced to and fro in the small room as he spoke, ignoring the low couch behind the door. Jan stretched out his legs, leaned back in his chair, and watched what he suspected was a prepared presentation.

"Suppose he really did go back; that he really is responsible for that Greenspan paper. He started out from a world in which that paper never existed, with all kinds of implications for how things had developed since the 1660s. In that world, Jameson didn't die in a flying accident, I've got an assistant called Ghislaine, and you decided to share your life with a girl who has now, in this location, never been more than a good friend. There could be countless other little changes, that we don't know about, even though, obviously, the broad sweep of history has stayed the same. But somehow, those changes are linked to the behaviour of the Portal itself. It opened two years early, and it delivered you, or Jan Two, or whatever you want to call him, back to the same time *relative to the moment when the Portal opened,* not relative to time in the outside world."

Jan thought about it. "It's a good story. Self-consistent. But why are there two of us?"

"Because of this shift in the Portal. You haven't gone through it, so you're still here. He has gone through it, and so he has come here."

"What happens to the pair of us in 1968?"

Matt's expression became serious. His body language still radiated tension and excitement, but he was clearly making a major effort to keep his words calm. Now, he did sit on the couch, leaning forward towards Jan.

"I've been thinking about that. It's why I wanted to talk to you alone. I've run some calculations through the Beast. It's pretty clear that having two versions of the same object—the same person—occupying the same interval of spacetime does put rather a lot of stress on the metric. The more particles there are involved, the bigger the stress. And there are quite a lot of particles in you. Both of you. The stress would be relieved, of course, if one of the versions were removed." He paused.

"You might think, since Jan Two comes from a world that doesn't exist, that he would be an anomaly, and ought to cease to exist himself when we get to the point in time when he stepped into the Portal."

Jan nodded.

"But you have to take account of the integration over histories. The way the actual path of a particle can be determined by adding up the probabilities of every possible path."

"Sure. That's smack in my period; goes back to Halley's work. Mathematically, you treat all the possible outcomes of an experiment as equally valid, but with different probabilities. The integration gives you predictions for the real world. Even though the ghost histories don't exist, you have to allow for what *would* have happened if they had existed."

"More or less." Jan could see that Matt wasn't entirely happy with his simplistic account, but that didn't stop the scientist from pressing on.

"See, the indeterminacy principle allows for the existence of ghost particles, constantly being created out of nothing at all in pairs, then destroying one another and disappearing back into the structure of space itself."

Jan nodded again. The story sounded vaguely familiar.

"And if you provide enough mass energy, in the form of a strong electric field, perhaps, then a ghost particle can be promoted into reality."

Jan could see where this was going. "You mean *he*," he gestured towards the window, "has been promoted into reality out of a ghost world using solar mass energy drawn off by the Portal?"

"I knew you'd understand. The snag is, when you do the integration, his history turns out to be stronger than yours. More probable. It doubles back on itself, you see, and that provides a very powerful reinforcement. Overwhelmingly powerful."

Jan looked hard at his friend, thinking it through carefully. He ticked the points off on the fingers of his left hand. First, the index finger went down.

"The spacetime fabric is under stress and wants to restore itself." It was Matt's turn to nod.

"The way it can do this is by eliminating one of the versions of me." A second finger was folded down.

"You can predict what will happen by integrating our histories." The third finger folded under his thumb.

"And that guy in there has a more powerful—a more *probable*—history than I have because he has doubled back on himself." The pinky disappeared into the fist, which Jan thumped into his right hand.

"Overwhelmingly more probable. Yes. I knew you'd understand."

"So what happens to me in two years' time? When he ought to be stepping into the Portal in his ghost world?"

"You go—somewhere. The calculations aren't precise on that point. My guess, and it's only a guess, is that you replace him in the ghost reality."

"Which means?"

"You cease to exist, for all practical purposes, and the Portal repays your mass energy to the Sun in exchange for the borrowing it made when Jan Two was created."

"So where is this other world?"

"Gone. Never existed."

There was a pause, while Jan tried to come to terms with the idea. Matt, after all, was the scientific brains of this outfit. MacNeil, for all his scientific background, was now just an administrator. And besides, his background was in ozone research, not fundamental gravimagnetics. Let alone, for God's sake, time travel. It would take something different from an administrator's brain to understand half of what seemed to be going on here.

It was too much to take in in one bite. But one thing was clear.

"The Chief will never believe it."

"Bugger the Chief."

Jan looked startled, made a vague gesture with his hands, rolled his eyes upwards, trying to point invisibly at any concealed devices. Hell, Matt was supposed to be persuading him that the guy next door was an imposter, that his story was a pack of lies. Whoever was listening in to this conversation must have their ears on fire by now.

Matt shrugged, waved his hand in a broad sweep. "There's nothing to worry about. Think I don't know how to set up a privacy shield? With Jean-Pierre's help, I admit." He tapped the pocket of his coverall. "Everywhere I go, the tell-tales go blank. MacNeil knows; everybody in Security knows. Does no harm—the pickups come back on when I go on my way. Without me, they've got no Project; without my shield, they don't have me."

Jan wondered just how reassured he should feel. To be sure, MacNeil hadn't yet come steaming in through the door. On the other hand, not being an expert himself, he wondered just how good Matt might be at electronic countermeasures, even with Jean-Pierre's help. It was not, after all, totally beyond the realms of possibility that the Chief might like Matt to *think* he had a working privacy shield, while biding his time to respond to his top scientist's little indiscretions.

Well, it was too late—or maybe too early—to worry about that now.

"OK. Bugger the Chief, then. But why do *you* take that guy's story at face value?"

"It's the simplest explanation that fits all the available facts. Ockham's razor—why complicate things if a simple explanation will do?"

"This is simple?"

"It's a damn sight simpler, Jan, than the notion that your double in there," he nodded towards the glass wall, "is some kind of spy. That stuff about plankton dieback—it rings true. There's *no way* it would be invented as part of a cover story. And besides, who'd want to try to hijack the Portal? The only people who know enough about the Project to be so well prepared are the people who are so keen to keep everything under wraps."

"So what do we do? How does this change things?"

"Why should it change things?"

Jan didn't reply.

"Come on, Jan, what difference does it make? Except that *we know the Portal works. We know we can change history.*"

"If you're right, he made things worse. Worse for the world, and a damn sight worse for me."

"So what? We can fix it."

An alarming image came into Jan's mind.

"I am *not* going to go back to sixteen sixty something and shoot myself with a trick crossbow dreamed up by MacNeil's special effects department."

Matt smiled, visibly relaxing for the first time since he had entered the room.

"It's a nice idea. I must admit, the thought had half occurred to me. But if that guy really is an alternate version of you, it would be too close to suicide for a well-balanced character like yourself to take seriously. And if I suggested sending back someone else to do the job, there might be complications trying to explain why I wanted you killed. And then, it wouldn't really solve the problem. You'd have to do the deed, avoid being arrested for murder, make your way to Winchester and then still have the job of persuading Newton that global warming is a bad thing. Which doesn't seem to be as easy as we once thought."

"Temporal inertia."

"Yes. But there are other ways in which you can eliminate Jan Two. Change history so that he doesn't exist—so that your history has the over-whelmingly high probability. And why not fulfil the real aim of the Project at the same time? We just need a better leverage point, some location where a change can't easily be damped out. We want to find a point where the flap of the butterfly's wing builds up as time passes—not into complete chaos, but enough to make a difference. And besides, there wouldn't be room for two Dr Thaddeus Greenspans in Winchester in 1668."

"You want me to go back further."

"Sure."

"How far?"

"Fourteenth century. John Borodin."

Borodin. The first real scientist. Discoverer of the inverse square law of gravity. The man who established the famous three laws of motion. Who explained the orbits of the planets around the Sun in terms of the same force that made an apple fall from a tree to the ground. But above all, the man who brought reason into science, who realised the importance of the analytical approach to complicated problems, breaking them down into simpler components that could be solved one at a time.

Norman French, Borodin had been. Originally Jean Buridan, but he had Anglicised his name when he came to Winchester. A loyal subject of the Empire, but he had brought Greek and Moorish ideas with him from the continent when he came to the great university in 1332—where, legend told, the discovery of the law of gravity was indeed stimulated by his observation of a falling apple. His genius had flourished in England, where the freedom to study such heretical ideas as the notion that scientific laws, not God, were responsible for planetary motions had been established since the time of Athelstan and his heirs, in the tenth century.

Even four hundred years after Athelstan, in the fourteenth century, the influence of Rome still held sway in large measure even in France, frowning upon too much freedom of thought. It was, after all, Harold's defeat of Duke William of Normandy, in 1066, less than three hundred years before the flowering of Borodin's genius, that had opened an English foothold on the continent, and started the spread of Anglo Saxon civilization across France. Without that civilising influence, under the unchecked reactionary religious influence of Rome, even a genius like Borodin could never have flourished in fourteenth century France. Science might have been set back for centuries.

Look at what had happened to Galileo. Even as late as the seventeenth century he had been persecuted by the Church in his native Italy, forced to flee to England, where he had occupied Borodin's old Chair at Winchester. How could he ever have developed his beautiful theory of relativity under the stifling hand of the Papacy? And where would Newton have been without the great tradition of Borodin, Galileo, and the other pioneering scientists of the Anglo Saxon tradition?

There were so few of them, Jan reflected; but each so essential. Great men, carrying the torch forward through the generations. Galileo himself had built on the work of Rene Descartes, who established the laws that governed the propagation of electromagnetic waves, the laws that revealed the fundamental constancy of the speed of light, the importance of which Galileo was so quick to grasp.

They had all applied leverage to history; butterflies flapping their scientific wings at crucial moments in history, when the world stood at the cusp, ready to tilt one way or the other. How many other geniuses had there been, whose ideas had gone unheard, failing to make a ripple in history, damped out by temporal inertia? The more he thought about it, the more the progress of science did seem like a succession of chaotic bifurcations, dramatic turning points that each came out of the blue, building on what had gone before, to be sure; but taking it off in unexpected new directions.

But it all started with Borodin. From the middle of the fourteenth century to the late eighteenth century, when Cavendish developed the definitive version of Newton's unified field theory, it had taken science just over four hundred years to develop a complete theory of the Universe, starting just about from scratch. Four hundred years, out of a human civilization spanning perhaps ten thousand years, starting from the time when our ancestors spread across Europe at the end of the latest Ice Age. It must have been wonderful to have been alive during those four centuries—and he'd missed the opportunity by such a small margin! Matt knew, better than anyone, how much Jan regretted being born a few centuries too late. That was why he had been roped in to the Project. But what did Borodin have to do with the present problem?

He voiced his bafflement. "What's Borodin got to do with it?"

"Suppose Borodin had never existed. Or hadn't discovered his laws. Or hadn't published. What would have happened to science?"

"There wouldn't have been any science, of course. At least, not in the fourteenth century. The time was certainly ripe for the discoveries, but

Borodin was a genius of rare insight; it might have been a generation, perhaps a hundred years, before anybody else did the work."

"Exactly. And isn't that what this Project is all about? Finding a way to delay the industrial revolution by a hundred years or so, giving time for the eighteenth century thinkers to realise the problems it might cause, and act before things got out of hand? Delay the scientific revolution, and you delay the industrial revolution. You can't tell me someone as bright as Cavendish wouldn't realise what was going on when it was happening right under his nose."

"Isn't this all a bit drastic? I mean, *Borodin* . . ." He thought for a moment. "And then, how can you be sure that Cavendish, or somebody, will realise the implications? Nobody did, in our history, until it was too late."

"Because it all happened so fast. Slow the pace of progress, and you inevitably give people more time to think the implications through. And I'm not asking you to kill Borodin. You know how cautious he was about making his work public. He sat on it for years before telling his colleagues; some of the optics wasn't published until after he died. And even then the gravity work was on the Catholic *Forbidden Index* for most of the next century. He knew just how controversial it was. Just find a way to persuade him not to publish at all. Frighten him with the Pope, or something. Suggest his work should be kept under wraps for a generation."

"It would be one hell of a change. What would I come back to?"

"No problem, Jan. Remember, now we *know* that history is subject to temporal inertia. Spacetime may be elastic, but the experience of Jan Two shows that it tries to shrink back into something close to its original state. If everything goes to plan, you'll come back to a twentieth century with a manageable warming problem, maybe a bit less sophisticated technology, but no drastic changes. In six hundred years, there'll be plenty of opportunity for history to restore itself in every respect except for the key change."

Jan seemed unconvinced.

"Of course, the bigger the change, the less scientifically advanced the world you come back to. There might even be some real science left to do—and you'd have knowledge, in effect, from the future."

"You cunning bastard. You know I'd give my right arm to be involved in some real science."

"You won't have to. Just three months out of your life. Three months to ensure that you still have a life to look forward to. Three interesting months in the fourteenth century. And you'd still have the opportunity to use the Portal again, maybe to drop a few hints in on old Newton. Because, after all, if this intervention works, old Jan Two in there, Dr Thaddeus Greenspan himself, will cease to exist. His whole visit to the 1660s will become a figment of alternate reality, leaving the coast clear for you." He smiled again, spread his arms expansively.

This was the bottom line. If what Matt had told him was true, Jan's only certainty of any existence more than two years into the future depended on finding a way to cut Jan Two out of history altogether. If reality really could only accommodate one of them, he had to take any steps he could to make sure it would be him. And those steps would surely have to involve the Portal. Matt's proposal might not be the only possible solution. It might not solve the world's problems at all. But off the top of his head, Jan certainly couldn't think of a better way to write Jan Two out of history.

"But what about you, Matt? What about everyone? Won't you *all* become figments of alternate reality?"

"If nobody knows anything has changed, what does it matter? I'll still be here. Maybe with slightly different memories. Maybe in a less scientifically advanced location, with opportunities to do some real work. Hell, if everything really is held up for a century, I could be the one to develop Maxwell's equations of gravimagnetics! They'd be in all the text books as the Evans Equations; a nice alliteration, don't you think?"

"You're crazy."

"No I'm not. Think it through. You know what it's like out there. Things are going to get a great deal worse before they get better, if they ever do get better. You make this change, and nobody will ever know but you, and the world will be a better place."

"And what if I end up like him?" Jan jerked his head towards the glass wall, beyond which his Doppelganger was now stretched out on the bed, seemingly asleep.

"He wasn't prepared. You will be. As soon as the Portal pulls you back, go through again without touching the colour pad—zero temporal displacement, a simple spatial shunt into the middle of the circle.

Then get the hell out of there. Remember, there'll be nice green grass, and trees."

"And Security."

"So? Just walk out. They won't bother a senior Project member *leaving* the site."

"Assuming there is still a Project."

"If there's no Project, there'll be no Security. For Christ's sake, Jan, I'm offering you a way out. A chance to avoid *certain* extinction in two years' time. You can't expect me to solve every little problem for you in advance."

He was right. A chance of life was better than the certainty of extinction. Jan suspected that there was something more, something Matt hadn't yet told him, but how could anything be personally more important to him? There usually was a sub-plot with Matt; but that didn't mean the version he presented for public consumption would be any less accurate. On matters like this, Jan trusted Matt implicitly. He'd tell you what you needed to know, and he'd tell you straight. The fact that he was also hiding something, and that Jan didn't know what kind of world he might come back to, were secondary considerations. But the chance that MacNeil might be eavesdropping their conversation, or might return at any moment, deserved more attention.

"OK, Matt. I'm not unappreciative. Really I'm not. When do you suggest?"

"Now. Your kit's already stored in the Portal chamber. I've added a priest's robe—acceptable clothing in any century. I want you out of here before any more copies of you turn up and complicate the issue."

"Is that likely?"

"Certain. Unless we move fast."

"You may not have noticed, but there's a Security alert on. The doors won't open."

"No problem. I've got a few more of Jean-Pierre's toys, some that MacNeil *doesn't* know about. Come on."

TWELVE

T HE DOOR OPENED SILENTLY AS MATT APPROACHED IT, ONE
hand buried deep in a pocket. The corridors were as empty as they
had been when MacNeil brought Jan into the Complex, but now he was
hurried along at a much brisker pace. Matt kept up a stream of talk as he
bustled Jan along.

"You see, if Jan Two can appear out of a ghost reality, so can Jan
Three, or Four, or Jan N."

This began to sound more like the subtext. They rounded a bend,
turned sharp left through another door which opened at their approach,
and began to descend.

"There's a finite probability that someone from one of the ghost
worlds closely resembling our real world will go back to interfere with
the past. The Portal promotes them into reality, they make the change,
and we suffer the consequences. The probabilities are small, but there's an
infinite number of ghost realities. You have to be first, go back furthest,
make the most clear-cut change. Then they don't get a look in—probability zero."

"Suppose *we* are a ghost reality."

"Don't even think about it. Besides, it doesn't work. All this stuff
around you is pretty real. Too much to make out of solar mass energy."

"Not enough elephants."

"Yeah. Not enough solar elephants."

The last section of corridor, although lined with metal, was much
more tunnel-like. It ended in a curved metal door, just like (the same as?)

the one described by Jan Two. Jan remembered his own first visit, when the walls had indeed been bare chalk. As far as he could remember, everything had been very much the way Jan Two had described, except for the presence of the fictitious (ghost?) Ghislaine. But he'd made so many visits to the Portal chamber since then that it was hard to remember the details.

This door didn't open at their approach. Cut from the wall of the construction housing the Portal, it depended upon old-fashioned human power. It was while Matt was swinging it open that they heard the approaching footsteps in the tunnel behind them.

"Damn." Matt had the door open now, gestured Jan to go through ahead of him. "I hoped we'd get more of a head start. But this should be enough."

Shouting from behind, MacNeil's voice, ordering them to stop, was shut off as Matt hauled the door shut, latching it in place with a simple metal bar.

He grinned at Jan. "I've been preparing for this, while you were flying down from York. Since MacNeil didn't believe Jan Two really came through the Portal, he was happy to seal this lot off without leaving armed guards inside. It'll take him a few minutes to realise that the door won't respond to any electronic requests. You'll be gone, and back, before he gets around to applying brute force."

They descended the steps down to the floor of the wedge shaped room, hurried through the door at the end and into the Portal chamber itself. Matt carefully shut the door behind them, although there was no means of securing it in place. There was nobody else there, but a large bundle, wrapped in brown cloth and tied to a wooden quarterstaff, lay to the right of the Portal.

"I don't think you ought to bother to change, Jan. I'm sure you can bury your clothes when you get through. And it ought to all come back with you, anyway. Everything you need is here, rolled up in the priest's robe. Just grab it, and go."

"Hold on, Matt." The silence behind them had given way to a dull pounding on the door; but clearly, if he wanted to, he could take two steps and be through the Portal before anybody could cross the outer chamber. *If* he wanted to. But did he? Matt had been hustling him along too fast since he'd dropped his bombshell about Jan Two. Maybe he ought to know a little more about this subtext. After all, *infinity* was a very large number. An *infinite* number of copies of himself? Wasn't there something here he ought to get straight?

"What's all the hurry? Even if you're right, at least let's wait until they break down the door. Give me time to collect my thoughts."

Matt picked up the bundle, pushed it into Jan's arms. "I really do think..."

Jan never found out what Matt thought. There was a sudden feeling of pressure in his ears, and a figure appeared on the other side of the Portal. Jean-Pierre had moved over by the left hand touch pad. He was yelling at Jan to get a move on, before it was too late. Matt was urging him towards the Portal, shouting in his ear.

"Yellow, Matt. Borodin. You know what to do. The more copies of you there are, the worse the strain."

The figure beyond the Portal was Jan's height, dressed for a 17th century winter, with long boots disappearing up under a greatcoat with its collar turned up, topped off by a black, broad-brimmed hat. That was all Jan could see from the rear view.

Urged on by Matt, with Jean-Pierre still yelling something indecipherable, he took a half step towards the Portal.

The figure turned. It was Jan Two. No, it must be Jan Three. From the expression on his face, he hadn't been expecting to be met by himself. He raised his right hand to his hat, sweeping it off to reveal a mass of unkempt hair, stepped forward as if to come through the Portal to Jan.

"Who the Hell..."

His words were cut off as Jean-Pierre crashed into him, knocking him to the ground, rolling the two of them clear of the Portal. Everything seemed to be happening in slow motion. Jan became aware of the sound of running feet, looked over his shoulder through the open door of the inner chamber to see MacNeil and a herd of Security types halfway across the antechamber.

There were tears, presumably of frustration, on Matt's cheeks. "*Please*, Jan. Before it's too late. We're on the edge of the cusp. It could go exponential."

An infinite number of copies of himself. A *very* large number of elephants. Whatever else it might do, draining all that mass-energy from the Sun would do more than dim it down a little. The bloody thing would go out!

"OK, Matt." He stepped forward, calmly, slowly. He seemed to have all the time in the world. Left hand on yellow. He had time to think, idly, how much excitement all this activity must be causing at the neutralino detector down in Switzerland. Right hand—he shoved the awkward bundle under his left armpit, hunching his body to wedge it in place. Saw a familiar looking back appear on the other side of the Portal, just as he reached for the right hand pad. The Portal flickered with purple light, and he felt a firm push in his back as Matt, rather unnecessarily, made sure that he went through.

1966 JUNE 22; 2.07 PM

On the dusty plain, the grass began to move. Swirling as if swept by a sudden whirlwind, it bent into patterns of interlinked circles. The shrubs swayed. But there was no breath of wind stirring the air, and the Sun still beat down from a clear sky. The vulture wheeled, attracted by the motion below, and dived to take a closer look.

In the underground chamber, as Jan stumbled towards the Portal three more copies of himself appeared in quick succession on the other side. Jean-Pierre disappeared, then re-appeared on the other side of the chamber, crouching at the console of a port-able computer. The lights started to dim, and a high pitched whine, on the edge of audibility, could be heard from the upper chamber.

Then, as Jan disappeared through the Portal, the whine stopped and the lights returned to a steady glow. Matt was alone in the chamber, checking the panel of the equipment alongside the Portal. On the plain above, everything was still in the afternoon sunlight. In the blue sky, the only sign of motion was the vulture, wheeling high above in its endless circle.

Thirteen

Rain, sleeting down from the northwest, soaked through Jan's coverall as he stumbled across the circle, falling to one knee as a result of Matt's enthusiastic push. He kept his bundle clear of the soaked ground as he rose to his feet and looked around him, wiping the rain from his eyes with his right hand.

There was precious little to see. The Stones themselves, low cloud, and a grey horizon. Anything interesting was concealed by the rain. But one thing was certain. This was *not* the plain of Sarum in 1966. The second thing that was certain was that he needed shelter, quickly. And he needed to change into dry clothing, and keep it dry, if at all possible.

The Stones themselves provided some protection from the wind, once he had found the lee of a suitably aligned pair. Could he *really* be in the fourteenth century? He looked up, ludicrously, as if he might be able to see one of Matt's hoverprobes. As if he would be able to see one in any case, if it were there, let alone obscured by cloud.

Once again, he wiped the rain from his eyes. Was it just the shelter provided by the Stones, or was it easing up? The brown robe around the bundle was beginning to look damp. Better to get changed now than wait for it to get really wet, he thought. C'mon, Jan; this is what you trained for. Maybe not *quite* what you trained for, but more or less. Get rid of the anachronistic clothing as quickly as possible, down to Sarum or some friendly farmhouse for shelter. Plenty of time to worry about Winchester, and Borodin, and all the rest tomorrow. After all, he had three months to sort something out.

The bundle contained long underwear, which clearly had no rightful place in the fourteenth century, but which nobody except Jan need ever see; two shirts, boots, leggings and a leather coat, obviously chosen by Matt from the seventeenth century kit; what seemed to be documents in a sealed, waterproof folder; and a pack of six survival ration bars. It also contained a leather pouch, secured by a drawstring, containing gold and silver coins. Jan ate one of the survival bars while changing. Matt, it seemed, wasn't desperately concerned about anachronism, no doubt trusting in Jan's judgement to keep things hidden, and to the Portal to bring everything back to the twentieth century in due course. The seventeenth century clothing might look a bit odd, but it would do until he could buy something more appropriate. The monk's robe was a masterstroke. Such fashions hardly changed from one century to the next, and he could surely pass himself off as a scholar from some distant monastery, visiting the University. He hoped the sealed folder contained further information from Matt, but he decided not to open it in the rain. It could wait until he found some proper shelter.

He bundled up the coverall, wrapping it around his light twentieth century shoes, and looked around. The ground was covered in a tough matt of grass, cropped short by some sort of animal (rabbits? sheep? nothing was visible in the misty rain), and he had no tools to dig with. To Hell with it, he thought. They're hardly any more incriminating than the underwear. He rolled the garment up more tightly, and tucked it out of sight under the robe. Pulling the hood over his head, he squelched off towards where the lane ought to be, assuming that the road he knew in the 1960s followed the path of the old lane.

He found a farmhouse a short distance down the lane. It was a low building, solidly built, with a thatched roof. Smoke rose from the chimney, and spread in a low plume to the southeast in the gathering gloom. He circumvented a noisy but unaggressive dog, splashing through the mud of the yard to the doorway, where a woman emerged, wiping her hands on a long apron.

The farmer's wife was hospitable, of course, in the Anglo Saxon tradition. This was a law-abiding country, with centuries of unbroken peace behind it. Her speech was intelligible enough, when he could persuade her to talk slowly, though laced with "thees" and "thous", and with a thick accent. Avoiding English as much as possible, sticking to the Latin which she seemed to get the gist of, if not the precise meaning, he explained that he was on a long journey, that he was Brother Sean, a monk from the monastery of Clonakilty, in the Erse kingdom, far to the west. A brief mention of a bad voyage from Corcaigh to Bristol was enough to evoke sympathy; he was happy to be back on land, he said, and so near his journey's end in Winchester, but he needed shelter for the night—a dry floor would do—and wondered if they could help?

The woman ushered him in to the single long room under the thatch. Two children, girls perhaps eight or ten years old, were sent to fetch bread for the visitor. Their mother explained that her surviving son was out in the fields with his father; that there had been another boy, but he had died of the plague. Jan expressed sympathy, but she seemed unconcerned. It was just one of those things, a fact of life.

Jan hoped that his shots were as effective as he'd been promised. The Black Death, he knew, had carried off—*would* carry off—more than one in twelve of the population of England during the second half of the four-teenth century, almost literally decimating the population. Cool, very wet weather seemed to have been an underlying cause, encouraging the spread of disease. It was one of the dips in climate that he had analysed—it seemed so long ago!—in that crazy paper with Matt. But it could have been a lot worse. At least the population in this part of the world had been spared starvation when the climate shifted, in the early part of the century, thanks to the organisation and planning of the prudent govern-ment of the Empire.

Even the well established farmers of England had been hard pressed by the change in the weather from the warmth of the previous century, and widespread starvation had barely been avoided by distribution of grain from central stocks. On the mainland of Europe, beyond the fringes of the Empire, there had been famine, and then the Black Death had struck—*would strike*, he reminded himself—in far more terrible fashion. During the next century, the hungry, depopulated lands beyond the Rhine would turn to the Empire for help, willingly submitting to Anglo Saxon rule in exchange for aid, and bringing the second (this time peace-ful) great expansion of its influence, leaving Italy, and Rome, in a Mediterranean backwater.

But all that was still to come, and here and now—in this *location*—the influence of Rome and the forces opposed to scientific progress might still, if Matt was right, be enough to persuade a wavering John Borodin to hide his light under a bushel for just another generation. He had ample time to mull things over, even after the return of the farmer and his son, thanks to the difficulty of maintaining any conversation in a mixture of the Latin which they did not understand as well as they thought they did, and the English which he professed not to understand as well as he really did. Warmed by the fire, fed a simple but sustaining meal, and largely left to his pious meditation, Jan spent a cosy evening and night. He said a few words to the farmer and his son when they appeared for the evening meal, slept (somewhat uncomfortably, but better than he had hoped) by the fire on a palliasse stuffed with straw, and left early in the morning, expressing genuine eagerness to be on his way.

The morning air was damp, and the sky still largely covered by cloud, but there was no real rain to hamper his journey. It was a long hike to Sarum, and he thought with envy of Jan Two and his ride on the land train, when he had come on a similar journey six months earlier, or three hundred years later, depending on your point of view. The thought made his head spin. If Matt was right, Jan Two never had made his loop through time, now. By the act of coming back to this location, and by the influence he would have over Borodin's plans for publication, Jan had altered reality so that Jan Two never existed, except as a vacuum ghost. He hoped Matt was right. A loop back six hundred years into the past ought to bloody well reinforce the strength of his own integrated history.

He was tired when he trudged into Sarum, an unprepossessing huddle of buildings but blessed with an inn and a few shops, where he was able to purchase appropriate clothing using just the smallest of the silver pieces Matt had supplied him with, and receiving a great handful of heavy copper coins in exchange. The professional people, the shopkeepers and the landlord of the inn, all spoke Latin, after a fashion, and he stuck to his story that he spoke scarcely any English, his native language being the Gaelic. Nobody seemed surprised. An academic priest, travelling to the great university at Winchester, might not be an everyday occurrence in Sarum, but was obviously nothing to get excited about.

It was, he established, the first week of September, 1366. Jan Two, he remembered, had arrived in the first week of September, 1666, according to the story he had told, and which Jan had no reason at all to doubt. Perhaps it was a rule with the operation of the Portal—step through in late June in the twentieth century, and you always arrived in early September in your chosen past century. Although of course, Jan reminded himself, it wouldn't be wise to draw general conclusions from a sample of only two time hops.

Whatever the reason, his arrival at this location was cutting things a bit fine. Borodin had died—would die—in October 1667. He hoped he wasn't too late. He hadn't done any detailed homework on the period—after all, he'd been expecting to visit Newton's location—and all he knew was that some of Borodin's best work had been published very late in his life. But the inverse square law of gravity, Borodin's law, he was certain was actually a posthumous publication. That, surely, was the key item, the one which he had to ensure was kept under wraps for a few more decades.

The documents in the waterproof folder, opened in the privacy of his room at the inn, proved disappointing. A personal note from Matt, wishing him well and stressing the importance of his task, and some scientific notes on Ockham's laws of planetary motion, including the insight that the orbits of the planets could only be explained as ellipses, not circles. He supposed it would come in handy; this work was little more than twenty years old, in this location (William of Ockham had died in the 1340s), and it was, after all, thoughtful of Matt to remind him how much he might be expected to know, here in 1366, so that he could avoid letting any hint of later knowledge drop. That could bring a disastrous end to his mission; the last thing he wanted was to *advance* the development of science and technology.

But there was little risk of that. Ockham's work would remain controversial, and widely unaccepted, until Borodin published his law of gravity. Even then there would be strong opposition from the still powerful, though declining, Papacy. For now (here in 1366), as Matt reminded Jan in his note, the notion that planetary orbits could be explained purely in terms of circles, with circular epicycles carrying each planet around its own centre of motion, while the centre of motion itself moved in a circle around the Sun, still held sway. The old idea, going back to the time of Aristotle, that objects beyond the orbit of the Moon had to move in perfect circles, because the Heavens were perfect—even if you needed two, or three, or more circles to explain one orbit.

Ockham had attempted to slice through this belief with his famous logical razor. If a single ellipse could explain the orbit of a planet, he argued, then this was a better explanation, because it was simpler, than one using several epicycles. But the famous razor, like the rest of Ockham's work, would only take its place in science in the wake of Borodin's discoveries.

Jan stayed for three nights in Sarum, acclimatising himself to the way of life and the patterns of speech of the natives. He was in no hurry, and happy to take time to begin to develop a passable fourteenth century English accent of his own, along with a few colloquialisms. Three months was ample time to get to Winchester and contact Borodin, and it was important that he should not seem too outlandish either in manners or speech. By the time he set off, dressed in genuine local clothes under his brown robe, with all the anachronistic twentieth century gear in a pack on his back, together with bread, cheese and a flagon of ale for the journey, and with a long staff in his hand, he looked every inch the monastic pilgrim.

Just over 215 hours after Jan had appeared in the Stone Circle, nine days later all but an hour, a figure dressed in a brown robe and clutching a small bundle stepped confidently out of nothing in the same spot. He walked purposefully to the edge of the Circle, and stood for a while, getting his bearings in the weak late afternoon sunshine. Then, he was striding briskly down towards the lane, and on towards Sarum. Passing the isolated farmhouse, he waved a greeting to the little girl, about eight years old, who was gathering eggs from under the bushes. She ran indoors, eager to tell her disbelieving mother that another pilgrim, just like Brother Sean, was passing down the lane. But he didn't stop. He knew where he was going, and was determined to get about his business as quickly and efficiently as possible.

It would not be until he got to Sarum that the brown-robed monk would hear disturbing news of an identically clad stranger, Brother Sean, who had passed that way just a few days before, and who spoke the same precise Latin and heavily accented English as himself. Keeping his hood well over his head, and agreeing that he was from the same order as Brother Sean, a fellow monk hurrying to catch up with him, the newcomer suited his actions to the words, pressing on into the grey night, in spite of offers of hospitality.

He was now more determined than ever to reach Winchester as quickly as possible, even if that meant sleeping in haystacks and eating the survival rations he had brought with him for emergency use. If this wasn't an emergency, what was?

FOURTEEN

EVEN IN THE FOURTEENTH CENTURY, ALL ROADS LED TO Winchester. Jan had no trouble making his way there, in spite of the atrocious roads and the persistent fine rain, which, he was repeatedly assured, represented a marked improvement over the recent weather. It was just under twenty miles, as the crow might fly, but perhaps half as long again following the road slightly to the north, around the rolling hills, before swinging back towards the city itself. Three days' easy travelling, some on foot, occasionally hitching a lift on a wagon, not hurrying at all, and continuing to get acclimatised. By the time he reached the outskirts of the city, nobody gave a second glance to the scruffy, unshaven monk, leaning on his staff as he looked down at the smoky huddle of houses below, lying in the lee of the great Cathedral.

The great Cathedral of St Peter and St Paul, very much as he knew it from the twentieth century, but without, of course, the additions made in the seventeen hundreds. There had been a great church on the site, originally known as the Minster, since it was first founded in the middle of the seventh century, by Cenwalh, King of Wessex. In 862, St Swithun, the seventeenth bishop, had been buried there, and in the tenth century the Minster had been rebuilt to become the greatest church in the kingdom, the Cathedral of a great See stretching from London to the Isle of Wight, a place of pilgrimage to the shrine of St Swithun, and the church in which the consecration and burial of the Anglo Saxon kings always took place.

But that great Minster church, for all its size and importance, had been almost entirely built of wood. Modern though it was, the entire structure had been completely rebuilt on the same plan but in stone at the end of the eleventh century, with even taller towers, in celebration of the triumph of Harold over the twin invasions from the north and the south. The defeat of Duke William of Normandy at the battle site near Haestin-gas in 1066 had marked the last time that a foreign invader set foot on English soil, and with Harold's enlightened rule the reign of the Anglo Saxon kings came into its full flowering. It was that rebuilt cathedral, completed in 1107, that Jan could now see in the clean simplicity of its original lines, uncluttered by the impressive, but inevitably obscuring, later additions.

The Cathedral dominated the city. From his vantage point on the hill to the north and west of the city centre, Jan could see the grid pattern of narrow streets to the north of the High Street, which itself ran almost east-west along the edge of the Cathedral Precincts. The city walls defined an inner region no more than a mile on a side, the heart of the old Roman town of Venta Belgarum. On this side, alongside him, high above the Westgate towered the Castle Hall, the seat of government; beyond it, he knew, lay the King's Palace. Outside the gate, a sprawling, higgledy-piggledy collection of houses spread out from the walls. To the north, there was chiefly open ground, and beyond the Cathedral and the Archbishop's palace, to the east, he could just about make out the swampy land beyond the river. But on the right, south of the Cathedral Close, be-yond the Southgate, lay what he was looking for, the University College it-self.

The University was nothing, of course, compared with the glory it would reach in another few centuries. By Newton's day, there would be six separate colleges, spaced along the bank of the River Itchen, each fronting on to the Kings' Gate road, and with extensive lawns at their backs, sweep-ing down to the river. Now, there was only the monastery, which would one day become St Swithun's College, and University College itself. Beyond, where the dreaming spires of Jesus College, Trinity, All Souls and Kings would one day rise, there was nothing but meadowland, grazed by sheep.

It all looked pathetically small and parochial, for the centre of a great Empire. Well, Jan told himself, at least it means I'll have no trouble finding someone like Borodin here. This may be the biggest pool of its kind in England, but he's an even bigger fish. Shifting his pack to the other shoulder, he set off on the last leg of his journey, through the Westgate and down the hill to the High Street, where the smoke from the chimneys promised him a warm and dry welcome.

It was raining again as Jan splashed down the High Street (actually a narrow lane, gloomy in the shadow of the shops and houses on either side), doing his best to avoid the filth from the horses, and the horses themselves. Almost at the edge of the Cathedral precincts, the market square opened out on his right, almost empty of traders in the late afternoon, but with a couple of women, bundled up against the weather, still offering a few eggs and some combs of honey for sale. Across the square, a painted sign showing the Sun being hidden behind the Moon indicated what had to be an inn. The sign of the Eclipse. Appropriate enough, for a traveller who had come here by way of the Stone Circle, itself an observatory used by the ancients in the prediction of eclipses—as Halley would prove in 1692.

The Eclipse offered a choice of ale or beer, surprisingly good bread, excellent cheese and cold meat that had seen better days as a snack to keep body and soul together until dinner time. It also offered running water, after a fashion—in a stone trough under a roofed cloister in the courtyard at the back. The same water, running on through a channel in the stone floor under the lean-to privy, also provided the sanitary arrangements. Jan didn't enquire where the water went next, but noted that it seemed to be flowing downhill to the east, towards the river. He made a mental note to keep well clear of the river itself, and to stick to the ale for drinking purposes.

The inn was owned by Edmund, a plump, perspiring and bald man, driven by his diminutive wife, who gloried in the name Aethelflaed, but responded to Ethel. A pot boy kept the customers supplied, and there were two girls who worked in the kitchen and did some desultory cleaning. They were also willing to wash Jan's clothes, almost coming to blows for the privilege in exchange for one of his smaller copper coins. He decided to rest up for a day or so and make himself more presentable before venturing across the Cathedral precincts to the University College.

Shaving, though, he had decided to abandon completely. Every adult male seemed to possess at the very least a luxuriant growth of moustaches and sidewhiskers, and the painful reality of cold steel dipped in cold water and scraped against a cold face on a cold morning had only served to bring home to him how far from reality his efforts in the comfort of his quarters back at the Project had been.

He waited three more days before venturing a meeting with Borodin. Cleaned up, his first visit had been to the great library, in a wing of the Cathedral. There, his impeccable Latin and evident scholarship had gained him access to the collection of manuscript books, each chained to its place on the shelves. With printing less than a hundred years old, these were still a working resource, pored over by other scholars, all under the watchful supervision of a grey-robed monk who sat on a high stool, surveying the room.

Long wooden chests under the windows contained, Jan knew, even older manuscripts, documents dating back at least to the seventh century, many of which would be lost between now and the twentieth century. He itched to get his hands on them; but the chests were double locked. Even in this location, their contents were valuable antiques, as well as historical records, and it would need more than a plausible manner and acceptable Latin to get permission for their perusal.

Borodin himself might almost be described as a valuable antique. On his second day as a visitor to the Cathedral, Jan had fallen into conversation, in the refectory, with a novice, Peter, who had been eager to offer his assistance to the visitor, showing him where to get food and drink. It was, he said, both one of the duties and one of the great pleasures of being a novice to look after the well being of strangers. Jan had explained his interest in natural philosophy, and over bread, cheese and ale they had discussed the relativity of motion, and what would happen to a stone dropped from the mast of a galley being rowed at speed across the sea. Would the stone fall at the foot of the mast, sharing the ship's forward motion? Or would it be left behind, and fall at the stern of the ship?

Jan was happy to discover that Peter was a confirmed Aristotelian, and favoured the latter view. He said nothing to dissuade him. Little chance here of a great leap forward in scientific understanding. Of course, Borodin's name had come into the discussion; and when Borodin himself entered the refectory (hardly a surprising coincidence, since it was, as Jan had carefully ensured, time for the mid-day meal), Peter had eagerly pointed out the great man himself.

Jan, however, had been taken aback by Borodin's appearance. He looked old—incredibly old, although he could only be in his sixties. For the first time, Jan began to wonder about the actual physiological ages of other people in this location. What was the life expectancy? Fifty something? He vaguely recalled something of the kind. Even allowing for high infant mortality, a man in his sixties, Borodin's age, really *was* an old man in this location! He was also a small man, slight in stature, stoop shouldered and with shuffling gait. But as Jan got over the first shock of his appearance, he noticed that Borodin's bright blue eyes were alert and intelligent, and that he constantly glanced around the room, taking everything in, noting the stranger and acknowledging his presence with a nod.

Yes, the novice confirmed, the great thinker was physically weak—had been, they said, since his brush with the plague, seven or eight years ago, though that was before Peter's time here, of course. He had come close to death, then. But God had spared him for a while, and his mind was not impaired. Naturally, the visitor would like to meet him, to discuss relativity of motion and other matters? Peter would be happy to make the arrangements. He knew the clerk who handled appointments for Borodin quite well, and Borodin was always eager to discuss his ideas.

So it was the following day, four days after his arrival in the city, and two weeks all but a day since he had stumbled through the Portal, that Jan was shown into Borodin's rooms by the clerk, another grey-robed functionary of the Cathedral, who stayed, seated at a desk on one side of the room, working on some documents. The room was on the ground floor of a cloister which ran along the eastern side of the main quadrangle of the College. It was built of stone, with a high ceiling and round-arched windows, and heated by a blazing log fire. Books and papers cluttered the floor, as well as the shelves that lined the walls and the surface of Borodin's own desk, under a window to the right of the clerk's desk. A heavy wooden door concealed more rooms—perhaps living quarters—in the suite.

Borodin had risen from his desk at Jan's entry, and escorted him, shuffling slowly, to two high-backed wooden chairs placed near the fire. In spite of the eternal damp outside, the room was dry, and uncomfortably hot.

"I hope you do not mind the heat, Brother Sean?"

He professed himself quite untroubled, but the blue eyes twinkled knowingly.

"My old bones, you see, feel the damp. I cannot be comfortable without the fire, and it does not seem to frighten all my visitors away."

"Any student of philosophy would put up with far more inconvenience than a warm fire for the privilege of discussing the nature of the world with you, sir."

"As indeed you must have, travelling so far, and by sea, at such a stormy time of year. I had not realised that I was held in such high regard, even in your part of the world. But then, the Erse have a tradition of scholarship. The tradition of Saint Patrick is still maintained, I believe."

This was a dangerous direction for the conversation to take. Whether out of misguided politeness or genuine curiosity, Borodin continued in the same vein. He seemed eager to learn all about the community where Jan was supposed to live and work, about conditions in the west in general, and about his journey to Winchester. Jan assured him that there was nothing at 'home' to rival the learning represented by the Cathedral here, the College, and by Borodin himself. Life was much like the life in any monastery, he supposed, and the weather was, if anything, even wetter than the weather here. He tried to make light of the journey, stressing that what effort had been involved was well worth the reward. He had come, he said, not to offer any new ideas to Borodin, but to find out as much as he could about the great man's own work, to take back and report to his colleagues. And, he thought, sweating under his robe not just because of the fire, if that doesn't get the conversation safely back onto scientific topics, I'm sunk.

Borodin smiled, gestured dismissively with his left hand at the repeated flattery. But he took the hint—after a fashion.

"Young Peter tells me that you are interested in the relativity of motion."

95

Jan sat quiet, wondering how to respond.

"Peter is a good boy, but sometimes his thinking is unsound." Borodin shook his head. "Of course, the stone will fall at the foot of the mast. If I were a younger man, and my bones ached less in the damp, I would ask the King to lend me a galley to demonstrate this. It would be a pretty experiment."

This was worse! As far as Jan knew, that experiment hadn't been carried out until the beginning of the fifteenth century. People had *talked* about it before—that was why he had felt free to discuss it with Peter—but nobody had actually *done* it for another generation. He hoped that Borodin wasn't really on intimate terms with the King, and prayed that an old man's forgetfulness would prevent the idea being discussed further. But he had an awful feeling that the mind behind those bright blue eyes didn't forget very much. Hastily, he tried to change the subject back to something safe and familiar even in this location. The one topic he had prepared, thanks to Matt's foresight in providing those papers.

"Actually, sir, I am primarily interested in the motions of the heavenly bodies. Ockham's work on the orbits of planets has caused great interest among my community. It seems to some to be heresy. It is, surely, more natural for objects to move in perfect circles, as Aristotle taught, than to follow the imperfection of these ellipses that Ockham talks about. Perhaps such ideas should not be discussed at all." Damn. He was handling this badly. All he'd wanted to do at this first meeting was get to know Borodin, prepare the ground for later. He still had about ten weeks here, ample time to build up to Ockham's work gradually. But in his eagerness to avoid discussing relativity of motion he was blundering on far too far, too fast, without preparing the ground.

"It seems to me that there may be some merit in what Ockham has to say."

The old man paused, looking into the firelight.

"But equally, I understand your caution. On balance, I think I would urge caution. You are, after all, a young man. Ockham is dead, and is unlikely to be troubled by any, ah, adverse criticism."

He was silent again, for perhaps half a minute. Jan wondered if the interview was over. Perhaps it hadn't gone so badly, after all, for a first meeting. Then Borodin stirred, looked him straight in the eye.

"I knew Ockham, you know. Met him in Paris; it must have been twenty-five years ago. We didn't always see eye to eye. But I don't think he would have been too worried about adverse criticism, even if he were alive today."

He lowered his gaze.

"It is different, though, for a young man, with no reputation in the world."

"You agree, then, that it is better not to discuss the implications of these elliptical orbits?"

"Implications?" Suddenly, the bird-like figure was all alertness, interest. "What implications are you thinking of? How advanced are your Irish philosophers with their calculations?"

"Why, I meant—" Jan tried to paddle his way out of the edge of the swamp he felt himself being sucked into. "The theological implications, of course. The suggestion that perfection might not rule in the Heavens. What else?"

"What else indeed." The old man looked back at the fire, seemingly involved in some mental debate, trying to make up his mind about something. Jan wanted to leave, but didn't know how to set about it politely.

"I could tell you about implications, young man, if you are what you say you are. Tell me, have you ever considered the fall of an apple?"

Jan was lost for an immediate response. Here was *John Borodin* himself asking if he had ever considered the fall of an apple! Every twentieth century schoolchild knew the story, even the ones who knew nothing else about science. But he could hardly say so.

"Why, no. Should I?"

"God chooses His own way to provide us with insight, Brother Sean. Some years ago, I nearly died of the plague. This feeble body has never been the same since that day. You may think that was a curse, a punishment, perhaps, for a misspent life. But it was while I was recovering from the illness that I spent many days, one summer, sitting out in the orchards where the apples which our monks so diligently turn into cider grow. I had occasion to watch many an apple fall from the bough, and little to do but think. One afternoon, I could see the Moon, quite clearly, between the trees, like some great fruit cast loose from the branches. I began to wonder why the Moon did not fall, like an apple, to the Earth."

He paused.

In spite of himself, Jan had to encourage him to continue. This was *Borodin*, recounting the anecdote known to millions from the preface to his famous posthumous book, *Principles of Heavenly Motion*, usually referred to simply from the shortened version of its Latin title, as the *Principia*.

"Surely, because it is in the nature of the Moon to travel in a perfect circle, around the Earth. It is easy to understand why an object should move in a perfect circle, but hard to imagine why it should want to move in an ellipse. As for apples, it is in the nature of apples to fall. They are as different from the Moon as chalk from cheese."

"And yet chalk and cheese both fall to Earth." Suddenly, a decision made, Borodin stood, pushing back the chair, and shuffling over to the shelves that lined the rear wall of the room. His clerk, Gregor, stopped scratching away with his pen and rose, asking if the old man needed any help.

"And yet, it does fall, you know." He was talking more to himself than to his audience, muttering in the way old men mutter when reminiscing about the good old days. "I have made some calculations, you see. You ask why a planet should want to move in an ellipse."

Jan couldn't quite remember, but he was sure he had asked no such thing. That was the one question he certainly had no intention at all of putting into the old man's head.

"I have solved that problem. Long ago, while recovering from my illness. It is a simple matter, once the mathematical techniques are understood." All the while he spoke, Borodin was moving papers, blowing dust off them, shuffling them into a new kind of disorder, brushing aside the efforts of Gregor to help. Suddenly he started towards the door to the inner sanctum, then stopped, turned towards Jan.

"I cannot find the papers now." A little petulantly, shaking his head in irritation. "But it is a simple matter, I tell you. And perhaps you know something of it."

Jan could say nothing.

"The Irish are a civilised race, after all. Come back tomorrow, and I will show you. Perhaps I have waited long enough. Perhaps it is time to share this information. Like Ockham, I will soon be beyond the scope of mortal criticism."

Gregor, standing just behind Borodin and with his hand on the old man's elbow, gestured towards the door with his head. Clearly, now the interview was over. Borodin was tired, becoming fractious. His physical frailty was more apparent than ever. Jan thanked him, promised to return in the morning, and left, closing the oak door behind him. My God, he thought, I hope I didn't get him too excited. What happens if he drops dead of a heart attack, more than a year too soon? Bound to change history in some unpredictable way.

Or would that be so bad? If Borodin died, here and know, Jan might be able to find his papers on gravity and destroy them. Surely that would achieve Matt's objective?

But even if Borodin survived the night, tomorrow he, Jan Ricardo, would get a chance to go over Borodin's gravity papers with the man himself! And, surely, with the subject out in the open he would be able to persuade such a frail old man of the wisdom of continued discretion. He'd sat on the work for nearly eight years, after all.

Convinced that things really hadn't turned out so badly after all, Jan was whistling as he returned to the Eclipse. The landlord greeted him outside the door, where he was supervising the unloading of barrels from a cart.

"Brother Sean!"

"Good day, friend. A very good day." He made to go in, but was stopped by a friendly hand on the arm.

"A surprise for you, Brother Sean. Another member of your order, arrived not two hours ago. He is in there now, eating his fill."

A friendly slap on the back urged Jan through the doorway, but he no longer had any thoughts of whistling. *Another member of his order?* It was impossible. Unless . . .

A tall figure in a brown robe, identical to the one Jan wore, stood warming himself at the fire, bent slightly forward, with his back to the door. As Jan entered, he straightened at the sound, but didn't turn.

"Ah. Brother Sean, I presume." He spoke perfect twentieth century English. "I'm so pleased to meet you at last. We have so much to discuss." He turned and stepped forward, hand outstretched in greeting. "Or should it be Brother Jan?"

It was Matt. Jan sat down, hard, on the nearest available chair.

FIFTEEN

"How did you get here? No, I mean *why*..."

They had repaired to Jan's room, on the first floor, overlooking the courtyard at the back of the inn.

"More to the point, Jan, *how did you get here?* You don't have to answer that. I think I know what's going on. But before we go any further, I ought to tell you that the last time I saw you you were being carried off on a stretcher with several broken bones and severe burns. The flyer bringing you in from York got caught in a gust and cartwheeled on landing."

An image of the helicopter, skimming the trees and levelling up at the very last minute, flashed into Jan's head.

"That bloody show-off pilot."

"Ah. You experienced something similar in your location, then?"

"Almost." The penny dropped. "But that means . . ."

"Yes. I am Matt, but I'm not *your* Matt. Obviously, you arrived more or less intact at the Project, about two weeks ago by your body clock, and my counterpart persuaded you of the urgent need to come back to this location and do something before the Portal went critical."

"Exponential, he said."

"Same difference. I had a different problem, you see. The simulations showed that everything was about to fall off the cusp, but I hadn't got a trained time traveller ready to send. Except—" he looked at Jan, expectantly.

"Except for Jan Two, or Jan Four, or whatever I ought to call him."

"Yes. Obviously our histories are *very* close to one another. Except for your counterpart. I'd have been quite willing to use him, if I could, but there was no way of spiriting him out of the care of MacNeil's mob. Especially not after what happened to you. Could've been sabotage, you see."

In spite of the turmoil in his brain, Jan noted Matt's choice of terminology. "Use him," he'd said. Just as Matt One had been willing to 'use' Jan? Well, it wasn't as if he hadn't realised. Even friends were experimental objects to Matt. But this Matt did seem even more cold-blooded about it than his own Matt had been. And he had to remember that to this Matt the real Jan was hospitalised back in 1966. It wouldn't do to rely on his friendship, that was sure. So why was he here?

"So you came instead. With my kit. Why?"

"Somebody had to. I waited as long as I dared, but there was nobody I could even discuss it with. All the indications were that something was about to blow, in a big way. So I came through. First got wind of you in Sarum. 'Another Brother from your Order,' they said, 'passed through here a week ago.' So I agreed, said I was hoping to meet up with you in Winchester, and managed to glean a few details about your cover story. Nice idea, that."

A disturbing thought had been taking shape in Jan's mind, stimulated by the image of his counterpart with the broken bones and severe burns.

"You're a ghost."

Matt frowned. "Well, we both are, I suspect. Figments of ghost histories, promoted into reality by the Portal, borrowing energy from the Sun."

"But *I'm* real. That whole world I came from can't have been made out of borrowed solar energy."

"But where is that world?"

Jan had no response.

"It doesn't exist, you see. Except as a potential. A *possible* history. Same as my world. You see—" he paused, looked thoughtful, spoke out again "—I've got the advantage over you, Jan. I've had a week to think this through."

You've also, Jan thought, got the kind of brain needed to think this through. But he kept quiet.

"The thing is, you see, we can't *both* go back. Perhaps neither of us can. There'll be just one reality, back in the twentieth century, corresponding to just one of our timelines."

"You mean we're rivals?"

Matt shrugged. "Sort of. Who cares? We've both got the same objective, I trust. Stop Borodin spreading the news of his insights into gravity and mathematics. If we succeed—if one of us succeeds—then we save the world for civilization as we know it. If not, we both lose out."

"You don't seem very bothered. I *mean*, if you're right, you might not be real."

Matt grinned, turning on the familiar charm. "Who cares? What is reality, anyway? It's just like life. First you don't exist, then you do, then you don't. The best you can hope for is to learn something, and have a bit of fun, in the middle."

Jan felt a chill on his back. He'd seen that grin when Matt—his Matt—had been twisting committees round his little finger. It might be genuine. Perhaps this Matt really didn't care what happened to him. Or maybe . . .

He decided to play along.

"It's just a bloody game to you, isn't it?" Jan spoke softly, shaking his head gently as he did so. "Just a bloody game. The whole thing. The Project, the Portal, gravimagnetics. Science. Life. Just a bloody game."

"Hey, Jan, come on. There's no purpose in life, you know. Even if we're real, we are only passing through. And this experiment is a humdinger. Suppose I have only got a real existence for three months, and some false memories of another few decades? How many scientists get a chance like this in a full three score years and ten?"

It made a crazy sort of sense. Matt really *was* the kind of guy who would be happy with his lot as long as it involved some wild scientific development. Even if that development rather curtailed his own life expectancy. But Jan certainly *wasn't* that kind of guy—so maybe he never would have made a decent scientist, after all.

And there was still that bottom line—however he'd got into this mess, Jan was stuck with it. No choice now but to follow through to its logical conclusion, or until he disappeared into a ghost reality. But he had to get one thing clear.

"You mean we can't go back? Not at all? That's not what you told me ..."

"Not what my counterpart told you. But I would have said the same. If you succeed, you will go back. Only it isn't really 'back'. You'll be promoted into permanent reality. 'Permanent', that is, as long as nobody else is monkeying with history. First thing you do when you get back, is shut down the Project. If you can.

"If you fail to sort out the Borodin problem, you drop out of the loop, somewhere. But if my calculations are right, and I assume my counterpart made the same calculations, or you wouldn't be here, you would've dropped out of the loop anyway, if you'd done nothing."

"So he said."

So there was a chance. Play his cards right, and he himself, Jan One, could get out of the loop. If it came to a choice, he resolved, he'd make damn sure that it *was* him, and not this smug bastard. Hell, this was, after all, only an imitation Matt. A much less likeable variation on the Matt theme than the one back home, Jan told himself.

They sat in silence for a few minutes. As far as Jan could see, he was on some kind of merry go round, and had no choice but to follow through with his original plan. If he succeeded, he'd be back in 1966—a different 1966, with no environmental degradation. And probably nobody he knew. But a chance to play a part in reshaping history. If he failed, in another ten weeks or so he would simply cease to exist. If he succeeded, this Matt, here, would cease to exist. No real loss. But how come Matt was here at all?

"I'm trying to sort this out, Matt. If I succeed in suppressing Borodin's work, your history won't exist, will it?"

Matt shrugged again.

"So doesn't the fact that you are here mean that I fail?"

"Not necessarily."

Matt fell silent again, seemingly struggling to make a decision.

"But probably. I have to admit it. The simplest explanation is that I come from the history that you create, as a result of your actions here. You change something, but not enough to make a big difference."

"Just enough to get myself half-killed!"

"Among other things. It's an interesting case. In theory, the correct procedure, if an attempt at reworking history fails, is to go back further in time to try to undo the mistake."

"That's what you—the other Matt—that's what you said. Avoid loops and paradoxes."

"Absolutely. If you make one mistake, don't get involved in that loop again. Go back further, and fix it so the loop disappears entirely, like your alter ego back in 1966."

"But, Matt, that would mean going back another three hundred years. To 1066."

"Yes. Given that we are restricted to using the Portal we know about. And that's just what *I* would have done, if I'd had any inkling that you would already be here. The differences between our two histories are just subtle enough to have us overlapping in this location. We need to compare notes carefully to find out what else is different. But, as I say, what you do here must change things enough so that my reality comes into existence. Then I come back, not realising that you are already here, to try the same sort of thing."

"Which doesn't seem to give you much chance of success, either."

"Well, I'll have a week after you've gone. Time to steal Borodin's papers and destroy them."

"You'll have to destroy him as well. The old man's still bright enough to reproduce the work again."

"Ah. You've seen him, then? Tell me about your progress."

Jan told him. Somehow, the way the story came out, it didn't look so promising as it had seemed earlier. And, after all, the very fact that he sat here, telling the tale to Matt (or an almost indistinguishable variation on the Matt theme) was a clear indication that things really had not been going as well as he had led himself to believe.

SIXTEEN

THINGS GOT WORSE.

They had agreed that Jan would keep his appointment with Borodin alone, mentioning that he had been joined in Winchester by another member of his order, Brother Matthew, who would like also to meet Borodin and discuss his work, at a later date. They hadn't wanted to appear to be ganging up on the old man, applying undue pressure. It might, Matt had thought, prove counterproductive.

If only he could have known! Jan needed all the moral support he could get at that meeting, and he wasn't getting any. Borodin had produced a small wooden chest, double locked like the archive chests in the library, which opened to yield a treasure trove of material, some on sheets of paper, some on rolled up scrolls. It was one of the scrolls, unrolled and weighed down with books at either end to stop it curling up again, that he displayed most proudly to his visitor.

Jan gazed with a mixed feeling of alarm and delight at the neatly inked drawings and careful lettering. The elliptical orbit of Mars, shown as tracing out equal areas in equal times at either end of the orbit; the apple falling from a tree, and the Moon in its orbit around the Earth, with arrows showing the direction and strength of the forces acting on them, and indicating the way their velocities must change as a result. And the famous calculation of the inverse square law, starting from the observation that an apple (or any other object) near the surface of the Earth falls through 16 feet in the first second of its fall and leading on through the fact that the Moon is 60 times further away from the centre of the Earth to the conclusion that the Moon 'falls' through a little more than one-twentieth of an inch each second, exactly the right amount of sideways nudge needed to keep it travelling in a closed orbit around the Earth, completing one circuit every month.

Borodin's enthusiasm seemed to have been fired by the interest of his visitor. He was delighted to learn that Brother Matthew would also like to discuss this work. With so much interest in the subject, and news having spread far to the west, he was sure, he said, that the time had come to publish. With the help of Brother Gregor, he would write a book. And if Brother Sean—and, indeed, Brother Matthew—had any advice to offer, then John Borodin would not be too proud to take it.

Except, that is, when the advice was to put everything back in the chest and forget about it. He brushed aside Jan's admittedly feeble attempts to warn him of the danger to his reputation of premature publication, the offence it might cause in the Catholic world, the possibility of the kind of bitter wrangle that might set back the cause of science for decades. Once, it seemed, Borodin had thought like that, had been afraid to go too far with his radical new work. He had put it in the chest under the bed, and all but forgotten it. But if the notion of elliptical orbits was being discussed throughout the Empire, it was time for his voice to be heard.

Everything suggested that Jan's efforts were having precisely the opposite effect to that he had hoped for. He might have tried harder—but the fact that Matt was here, in this location, removed much of the incentive. He *knew* that his mission must fail, or Matt wouldn't be here. So why bother going through the motions? His objections became feebler still, as he luxuriated in the pleasure of having what amounted to a private tutorial on the discovery of the inverse square law, from John Borodin himself.

After all, if his mission here in 1366 was destined to fail, there was only one choice open to him. Matt himself had pointed the way. A half-baked plan began to develop in Jan's mind.

Over the next few days, the plan began to take shape. After introducing Matt to Borodin, Jan allowed himself to slip into the background, and, as often as not, stop attending the regular meetings between the two scientists. Matt professed dismay at the way things were going, and his inability to convince Borodin that discretion might be the better part of valour. But Jan doubted that he really had his heart in his work. Like Jan, he was seduced by the opportunity to live through a key development in the history of science. Perhaps, like Jan, he was beginning to think of alternative possibilities.

Jan had the edge—a week's edge. But he only had the edge provided he was out of harm's way. If anything happened to him—and a broken leg here could be as serious as a flying accident in 1966—Matt would have the opportunity to seize control of the situation.

Although chiding himself for his paranoia, Jan began to be increasingly cautious in his dealings with Matt. He declined an offer to share a room—why bother, he pointed out quite reasonably, when they had more than enough gold to buy the whole inn, if they'd wanted to? It might not be quite in keeping with their cover, but they'd be well out of reach of anybody here before anyone in this location could get really curious about them. And it might fit better with Jan's developing plans. He took his meals separately, whenever he could reasonably do so. And he was most particular not to let Matt know what exactly it was he was researching in the chain library.

Like all librarians, the old monk in the grey robe liked nothing better than to talk about his charges. He wasn't very keen on them actually being read, let alone taken out of his sight, but he was happy to spare you the trouble of reading them yourself by talking about them, and their history. There were books in the library more than seven hundred years old; but the monk, Aethelred, was proudest of the tenth and eleventh century volumes, from the time of Athelstan, Harold, and Edgar the Atheling. He brushed aside the short-lived intervention of Cnut and his sons, from 1015 to 1042, as an insignificant hiccup in the growth of Anglo-Saxon glory. And he was happy (as happy as he was to let anybody touch his treasured manuscripts) to let Jan pore over the accounts of the Battle of Haestingas, in which Harold had defeated William of Normandy and secured the crown, first for himself and then for Edgar, the grandson of Edmund Ironside and the great grandson of the librarian's namesake, Aethelred.

Jan's plans had taken firm shape, and he was ready to make a move. But one thing puzzled him, and he might never get a chance to discuss it again. He broached the subject after dinner, sitting in one of the high-backed chairs, close against the fire. A flagon of wine, now empty, had been passed between them several times. Jan had been careful only to sip at his beaker, while Matt gulped down his share; this was totally out of keeping with the Matt Jan knew, but this version seemed fond of his tipple. All to the good.

"Don't you think it's strange that the Portal always seems to open on key moments in history? Out of all the years it could open up on, we've had access to the 1660s, when Newton was alive, now, when Borodin was laying the foundations of the scientific method—even the 1960s could be regarded as a turning point, with the environmental problems."

"And further back." Matt puffed on the china pipe that he had taken up a couple of days ago. His hair and beard were greasy, and there were stains on his robe. Jan thought this might be taking his attempt to blend in with the local community a little far, but said nothing. The Matt he'd known had been untidy, but not a slob; this Matt was an altogether less savoury version, and would be no loss at all to the world. But his brain seemed to be every bit as good as that of Matt One. "Another 300 years, and you've got the beginning of Harold's reign, the first movement of the Empire onto the continent. The seven hundreds, and the Norse voyages to the New World."

"D'you think it was set up that way?"

Matt shook his head. "More likely, there's some significance about these locations. Places where the spacetime fabric is weak, susceptible to change. That's what makes it possible to open the Portal here."

"It doesn't seem very susceptible to the changes we want to make."

"No. But you can't deny we've changed old Borodin's life."

Jan sat for a while, watching the flames.

"Why should the spacetime fabric be susceptible at precise three hundred year intervals?"

There was no response.

"A lot of the turning points in history are linked to the climate changes—the cycle of mini Ice Ages."

Matt laughed, not altogether pleasantly. "Still riding that old hobby horse? Sometimes I wish I'd never let you talk me into writing that paper."

Jan stifled a sharp answer. The fat bastard needn't think he was going to needle Jan into an argument.

"You've got to admit it makes sense. Spells of severe weather act as a stimulus to scientific progress, encouraging new ways of thinking, new ways to tackle old problems. Anything that shakes society out of its rut encourages new ideas to spread."

"You're crazy. How would that fit in with the locations of the Portal? Surely you agree it can't be just a coincidence. It's more likely to be leverage. There are natural places in the fabric of spacetime that provide fulcrum points, and that's where the Gate opens. So, obviously, events at those locations determine the overall shape of history."

In spite of himself, Jan *was* getting annoyed by Matt's arrogant self-confidence. "I don't know," he muttered. The urge to put one over on Matt grew.

"Why should the fulcrum points be at 300 year intervals?"

Matt smiled, like a teacher humouring a dim pupil. "Why not? Show me something in the spacetime equations that says it can't be so."

He knew Jan couldn't argue about the maths. God, it was cold tonight. Jan stretched his feet out to the fire, declining to answer. A thought struck him. Was it a moth or a butterfly? He drank some wine from the beaker held in his right hand, and chased the thought around his head for a few minutes. It might make sense.

"Matt?" His companion seemed to be dozing, his own glass empty on the floor beside his chair, pipe cold in his hand. He stirred at the sound.

"Uh?"

"Matt, *suppose it really is the Portal that causes the climate change.*"

Matt opened both eyes, looked intently at Jan. The urgency in Jan's tone had obviously got through to him. This wasn't the arrogant charmer, this was Matt the scientist, suddenly sober and alert.

"You remember—that is, I imagine you must have had similar discussions back in your original location. The Portal drains off power from the Sun while it's open. What were the figures—up to a ten per cent reduction over 30 years or so? Every 300 years?"

"Maybe a bit less." In spite of the dismissal, he could see that Matt was hooked.

"Well, in round numbers. Matt, that means a 1 per cent reduction overall. Ten per cent of the total, for ten per cent of the time. That's not peanuts. Where does it go?"

Matt fumbled for his glass, picked it up, looked at it, dumped it back on the floor.

"Maybe the Portal needs that much energy to run on."

"Be serious, Matt. *One per cent* of the Sun's output, stolen from it over a span of, what, 50 thousand years, if we assume the Cavendish time sets a limit. *Where does it go?*"

"Only one place it can go. Into the future."

"Why?"

They sat silent for a while. Then Jan leaned forward, gazing intently at the now fully alert Matt. "Try this. When is the next Ice Age due?"

"On the basis of the geological cycles?"

He nodded.

"About six thousand years from now. Maybe less. But that's assuming the pattern of the past million years repeats."

Jan waved a hand, dismissively.

"It's held up through ten cycles, why should it stop now? But just think, Matt—if you stole 1 per cent of the Sun's output over fifty thousand years, you could provide a fair bit of extra heating when the world got cold. Maybe an extra 10 per cent over five thousand years. More over a shorter period."

"You think that's what it's for?"

It was a beautiful idea. Jan looked at it in his mind from all directions. He liked it more the more he thought about it. Like all the best scientific ideas, it had sprung out of nothing at all, his idle speculation about the significance of the locations on which the Portal opened. He could see that similar thoughts were going through Matt's head. Knowing Matt, in a few minutes he'd be convinced that it was all his own idea, and that Jan had merely filled in a few details. Let him think that. Jan knew whose idea it was, and he knew it was right. And in any case the arrogant bastard wasn't going back to 1966, not if Jan had anything to do with it.

"I think. Wish we could test it, but it makes sense. Somebody, up ahead five or six thousand years, is getting cold. So they built the Portal to pull in a bit of heat from the past—at the expense of creating a few mini Ice Ages at intervals down the line. They're stealing heat from the Sun *now* and using it to make the world warmer *then*.

"And those mini Ice Ages provide the punctuation marks in the growth of civilization. So inevitably, anywhere the Portal opens is going to be a leverage point in history."

"Not bad. It even makes sense out of your old ideas about climate and history. Pity you won't be able to publish it."

"Yeah. A real shame."

He leaned back in the chair, closed his eyes. To Hell with publication. He had other things to worry about. But it gave a boost to one thing that concerned him. If there was anything in this idea at all, it meant that 1066 would be a turning point. Not so much because of the actions of any one individual, but because the changing climate caused by the Portal itself would encourage movement of population, make peasants restless, make governments take action to keep things under control. No more pussyfooting around. It *had* to be a turning point, or the Portal wouldn't open there. And this time, he would make damn sure that things turned in the direction he wanted them to turn.

Security at the University College was non-existent. Jan had to go out of his way to make sure that a brown-robed figure was seen slipping into the cloisters while Borodin and Gregor were at the evening meal. He could rely on no alarm being raised until the morning, by which time he would have a good start, and time to extend it during the confusion of the false trail he intended to lay.

He had waited another four days before making his move, partly out of fascination with everything he had found in Winchester, partly, he had to admit, from nerves. But it was now mid-October. Frosts were hardening the mud of the roads, making conditions briefly easier for travelling, before the winter proper set in. He had little more than a month before he would be unceremoniously yanked back to 1966 by the Portal, and he had a lot of travelling to do in that time. He needed to put as much distance as possible between himself and Winchester.

But first he had to muddy the trail behind him, and make sure that Matt didn't get up to any tricks that might rub Jan's history out of the probabilities entirely.

The door to Borodin's rooms was locked. The lock was a massive affair, almost big enough for him to stick his fist in the keyhole, and he could probably have picked it with a crowbar. But there was no need, since the shutters closed against the window looking out on to the cloister were not locked at all, simply secured with a slim wooden bar, designed to keep them shut against any stray breeze that might blow their way, not to deter a determined burglar. Reaching in through the crack between the shutters with the end of his staff, Jan levered the bar upward, until it came loose from its sockets and fell with a clatter on the stone floor inside. He looked around, ready to melt into the shadows if need be, but nobody came to investigate the noise.

Once inside, he moved swiftly to gather the papers he wanted. His dark adapted eyes could see well enough by the flickering light from the hearth, where the fire had been left burning untended in the grate; nobody, especially an old man with aching bones, would let his fire go out at this time of year, if at all. Most of the papers were still on the table, where he, Matt and Borodin had been studying them that afternoon. Borodin's chest, with the double locks, was open on the floor beside it. Without bothering to check through the documents, Jan picked a heap of them up in his arms, and dumped them on the fire. The temperature in the room seemed to drop five degrees as the warm glow was cut off by the heap of paper. Then, smoke began to rise from the edges of the pile, followed by flames licking across the documents, lighting up the room brighter than before. But Jan paid no attention.

Back at the table, he was looking at the scroll containing Borodin's beautiful exposition of the inverse square law. He had to have some evidence to plant on Matt, and this was the best bet. But should he take the whole thing? If he did, it would leave Borodin with his complete masterwork still intact. On the other hand, if he burnt half of it, it wouldn't look right.

While still debating with himself, he heard footsteps outside, passing along the cloister. Could dinner be over already? Time to get out. Without thinking further, he rolled the scroll up, and tucked it into the sash holding his trousers up, beneath the brown robe.

At the window, he glanced both ways. Two grey robed backs were disappearing to the left. He waited until they turned in at the staircase in the corner of the quadrangle, then he was through, pulling the shutters to behind him and scurrying off to the right. At the College gate, while keeping his hood well over his face (reasonable enough, in this weather) he made a point of bidding good night to the monk on duty in the little watch room—on duty not to keep intruders out of the College, but to provide assistance and welcome to visitors.

He slipped and almost fell on the way across the Cathedral Close. The frost was coming down hard and early tonight, from a rare clear sky. He hoped the horse would be able to cope alright. The bloody horse was not exactly the weak point in his plan, but certainly the bit he was least comfortable with. Sure, the Project had insisted on giving him riding lessons, just in case. And, sure, the lumbering great beast, more carthorse than thoroughbred stallion, that he had picked out and paid for at the stables that morning, seemed placid enough. But it was a hell of a long way to fall from the top of one of those great brutes to the ground, and the ground was going to be uncomfortably hard tonight. He consoled himself by pondering the irony that Matt's had been one of the most insistent voices urging the riding lessons on him, back in the 1960s; now, Matt was going to have to suffer the consequences. And the best thing was, Jan knew that Matt couldn't ride at all.

At the inn, he slipped straight through the smoke-filled fug of the public room, nodding at Matt on the way. Matt, as usual, was three parts down a flagon of wine by now, having eaten his fill. You could tell he had eaten from the state of his beard. You almost had to admire the way he blended in with the natives. Except that it had become only too obvious that this Matt was a natural-born slob, and wasn't acting a part. Even so, usually at this time of night Jan would join him by the fireside for a drink, tolerating his slovenliness for the sake of some twentieth century conversation. But tonight, after visiting the privy Jan didn't go back into the warmth of the public rooms. Instead, collecting a candle lantern from the kitchen, he went up the back stair to the bedrooms.

His pack was ready, under the bed, away from prying eyes. He got it out, placed it by the door. But before he left, he proceeded to rip the place apart, as quietly as possible—gently overturning the chair and table, laying them soundlessly on the floor; pulling bedclothes off the bed; opening the chest beside the bed, and strewing most of the clothes he had bought around.

It took only a couple of minutes to slip out of the robe and change from fourteenth century underclothing back into the garments he had been wearing when he stepped through the Portal. Robe back in place on top, pack and staff in one hand, scroll tucked into the cord that served as a belt around the robe, he stood by the doorway, nodding as he surveyed his handiwork. Now for Matt's room.

Two doors down, on the same side of the corridor, he listened at the door for a moment before pushing it open, almost dropping the lantern as he fumbled with the latch and his several burdens. It was OK. As he'd expected, Matt was still dozing by the fire downstairs. Now, where would be the best place? It had to look as if it was hidden, but it had to be easy enough to find. Though there was bound to be a fairly thorough search of Matt's room, surely, when they saw the mess in his own room?

He settled for slitting a seam of the horsehair mattress with the impressive knife that had been one of his first acquisitions in this location, and which had since come in handy for everything from cleaning his fingernails to eating dinner. He stuffed the scroll in, taking care to dribble some of the horsehair out in the process, then replaced the bedcovers. It wouldn't take much detective work to find that. He was set. Time to go.

But as he straightened up from re-arranging the bedcovers, leaning on his staff and already reaching for the pack he had left at the bedside, he heard a step outside, and then the door opened behind him. He turned, quickly, to see Matt, blinking in the candlelight.

"What's up, Jan? Looking for me?"

Damn. He had no choice. Even as he stepped forward, Jan told himself that it might actually be for the best. Would certainly make it look as if the two of them had been up to no good and had fallen out.

"I'm sorry, Matt." Sweeping the staff round in the approved manner, he swept Matt's legs from under him. He hit the floor with a crash, but immediately flung himself at Jan's legs, clutching them in a bear hug that brought him also tumbling to the floor. Drunk Matt might be, but incapable he certainly was not.

Shaken by the fall, concerned about the noise and the possibility that at any minute someone else might burst in, totally ruining his plan, Jan began to fight back in earnest. He was not going to get his leg broken and be stuck in some ghost time loop while Matt breezed off back to 1066 and rewrote history.

The bedclothes had come down with him, somehow, when he fell, tangling round his lower body and Matt's head and shoulders. They were doing as much as Matt himself to impede Jan. But his right arm was free, and the dagger, which had been lying on the bed following his surgery on the mattress, was within reach. Grabbing it, he held it with the blade upward, and brought the hilt down hard, twice, on the lump under the bedclothes that corresponded to Matt's head. Matt stopped moving, and lay inert, across Jan's legs.

Struggling to free himself, Jan had time to hope that he hadn't caused any permanent damage. He didn't really wish Matt any long term ill, even though he was about to write him out of history and send him back to the ghost reality that he had emerged from. Let the old bugger have as good a time as possible in the few weeks of existence he'd got left. But first things first—which meant looking after his own timeline.

Panting, he stood for a moment looking at the mess. It was even more spectacular than his own room, with a body—a groaning body, he was relieved to note—as well. The mattress, oozing hair, was an obvious place for anyone with normal curiosity to probe. But there were more sounds outside, footsteps on the stair. Pulling bedclothes out of the way, and noting with slight disgust that Matt seemed to have pissed himself, Jan grabbed the pack and staff, and stepped to the window. Flinging open the shutters, he looked down. The roof of the privy was just below, and there was nobody about. Pack and staff were quickly dropped to the ground, then he was through, dropping onto the sloping roof and sliding down to join them.

He was out of the courtyard before the sudden hubbub from the lighted window showed that his handiwork had been discovered, and picking up his horse from the stables before Matt was alert enough for anyone to begin to understand what had been going on. The state of Jan's room convinced them that both monks had been the victims of robbery, at least, and that Matt's confused mention of a fight suggested the worst had happened to his compatriot. The confusion was compounded by Matt's inability to remember exactly how he had come to be lying on the floor in a tangle of bedclothes, with a splitting headache.

If Jan could have known, he would have been delighted at the muddy state of the waters he had left behind him. But while messengers were being sent to the College to find somebody who could explain the significance of the obviously valuable scroll that had been concealed in Brother Matthew's bed, and which presumably the unknown intruder had been attempting to steal, Jan was already mounted on his trusty (he hoped) carthorse, plodding out of Winchester on the road east, worrying about the possibility of a pursuit that would never, thanks to Matt's amnesia, materialise. He had warm clothing, some food, plenty of money, a horse and a large knife. He would need all of them in the weeks ahead; he had only a vague idea of the route he intended to follow, but several weeks in which to carry out a reconnaissance that would, he hoped, stand him in good stead three hundred years ago, in 1066.

SEVENTEEN

B Y THE END OF NOVEMBER, JAN HAD DEVELOPED A respectably bushy beard. His hair was long and matted, he'd lost weight, and he'd become much more skilful with the knife. Even though he had taken advantage of any hospitality that might be on offer to a ragged wandering monk on some obscure pilgrimage, there had been enough nights sleeping in barns alongside the horse, and enough days when he'd been glad to supplement his diet with the flesh of some small mammal caught in the hedgerows or under the trees, and roasted on an open fire (for which, every time, he thanked Matt One, wherever he might be, for including that lighter in the bundle) to make him unrecognisable from the clean, comfortable figure that had come through the Portal almost three months ago.

Almost three months. He'd made it as far as Hleaws, a small town on a hill, overlooking a river, but still probably two days fairly stiff travelling, or three at his leisurely pace, to Haestingas. He hadn't been pressing hard, but the journey had taken longer than he had expected. The horse was every bit the plodder he had seemed at first sight, for which Jan had been thankful in the early days, but which had become, as his experience with this form of locomotion increased, increasingly irritating; and he was beginning to worry on two counts. First, that he would be snatched back to 1966 in his sleep, unprepared. He couldn't remember, if he had ever known, the exact length of time he was allowed here. And in any case, he wasn't sure, to the exact day, how long he had been here. So he could be snatched back any time, now.

To that end, he now wore his long underwear, two shirts, twentieth century coverall, leather coat, boots and robe at all times, except when calls of nature unavoidably required that some of his garments be removed. He slept like that, bundled up in a sheepskin rug that he had acquired in Twyford, and with the knife in a sheath tied to his left forearm. He knew there was little chance of the knife travelling back with him; only original twentieth century organic material, Matt had said. But maybe Matt was wrong—or maybe, for reasons of his own, he had been lying. Jan no longer took anything at face value.

His second concern was how long the journey had taken. He had his deadline to meet—14 October, 1066. The records in the chain library had been quite clear, as well as giving full details of the battle. If he was able to get through the Portal again, he could expect to arrive in the first week in September. Barely a month to complete the journey, in the cold, on rutted tracks, in the short hours of daylight. How Harold's army had managed—would manage—to march 270 miles from Stamford Bridge to Haestingas in seven days he would never know. Travelling at half that speed was about the best he could manage, on a good day. And he would need time to establish his cover and find a way to put his cherished plan into operation.

For, as Jan was well aware, the great snag with his plan was that it didn't suggest exactly how he was going to be able to alter the outcome of the Battle of Haestingas. He just knew, with more force than he had believed anything in his life, that if Harold were to lose that battle then the growth of the Anglo Saxon Empire would be set back for decades, perhaps a generation. If it took the English an extra fifty or a hundred years to begin to establish their European Empire, it would take that much longer for the scientific and technological revolutions to get started. Ideas about relativity of motion would have to wait; Ockham might never come up with the idea of elliptical orbits; Borodin would not be led to speculate about gravity, and the discovery of the inverse square law might have to wait until the fifteenth century. Surely *that* would achieve the original aim of the Project, slowing the pace of change and giving later thinkers, like Galileo and Newton, a chance to appreciate the dangers of change?

And, more to the point, he was bloody well sure that it would write Jan Two and his little timeloop out of the histories, since the Newton Jan Two had visited would no longer exist. Would *never* exist.

The bottom line was, all Jan really cared about any more was the survival of Jan. Although the historian in him did sometimes wonder, during the long nights huddled in a barn, how things might turn out. Just who would notice the ellipticity of the orbit of Mars? Which great thinker would decipher the inverse square law? With everything set back a hundred years, it might be Newton, perhaps, who would solve the electromagnetic equations. Or maybe science would take a different tack altogether, making new discoveries or seeing the discoveries he was familiar with in a different light.

If it really was a question of leverage, and flapping butterflies—falling off the cusp, as Matt (which one? he couldn't remember) had put it—then no wonder science proceeded as a series of revolutions. And the one predictable thing about revolutions is that their outcomes are not predictable. If all went well, he would be able to spend many a happy hour reading the history books of the location he ended up in, and comparing the story they had to tell with the history he remembered.

One thing was sure. The world of 1966, his ultimate destination, would be a simpler place as a result. But to get to that simpler version of 1966, he had to go the long way home.

The opportunity didn't come, as he had feared, while he was asleep, or while he was squatting behind a bush with his trousers round his ankles. It came on a misty evening as he stood alongside his horse, looking up at the walls of Hleaws. It would be simpler to trudge on a bit further, find a farmhouse to stay in for the night. Farmers seldom asked questions, especially if you offered to help with some of the chores, but in the last two towns he had visited Jan had been uncomfortably aware that his appearance was by now distinctly out of the ordinary. On the other hand, the west gate of the town was here in front of him, and night was falling. There would be inns inside, and he still had some silver pieces to jingle in his pouch.

He was spared from making the decision.

In front of him, there was a blank wall. The pale pink light made it difficult to see, and the heat was almost overpowering. But he had known this would happen some time, and he was ready.

He could tell from the lightness of the sheath attached to his arm that the knife was gone, but the wooden staff that he had been leaning on was still in his right hand. He whirled, and leaped straight back through the Portal, not waiting to check out who was there before he leaped. It was only during his leap that he took in the brown-robed monk, clutching a long metal staff and a misshapen bundle, staring at him in astonishment.

Did I really used to be so fat, Jan thought, baring his teeth in a wild grin. Time seemed to go into slow motion; he had time to take everything in before his feet hit the ground again. Matt was to one side, his back half turned on the Portal, talking to a woman—a girl, really—who crouched by a stack of electronic equipment. Another man was just closing the door on the other side of the chamber.

Then he hit the ground, and everything went into fast forward. Jan struck his counterpart in the stomach with the end of the staff, kicked his legs from under him as he dropped the metal staff and the bundle to clutch at his midriff. Matt had turned, made a grab for him; the woman was rising, moving into action; the man stood, transfixed, at the door.

Green, Jan said to himself, as he turned to meet Matt's charge, jabbing the staff towards him. *Green for the eleventh century*, as Matt grabbed the end of the staff, tried to use it to twist Jan off his feet as he stumbled forward. He let go of his end of the staff. This was a mistake. Matt, yelling something, in which Jan only caught the word "exponential", immediately swung it into an attack position, moved forward.

Shit, Jan thought. *No bloody time*. The odd-looking metal staff that his groaning counterpart had dropped was right at his feet. Jan bent, ducking under a swishing blow from Matt's staff, and grabbed it. It wasn't a staff at all, he discovered, but some sort of projectile weapon—a long tube, with a weighty, bulbous end. The weighty, bulbous end made a satisfactory crack as it struck the head of his attacker. He reversed the tube, ready to jab the woman away as Matt fell to his knees. But she was already backing away, hands half raised. "Be careful . . ."

It definitely must be a projectile weapon! The guy at the door had it open now, was shouting through it for reinforcements. The girl was out of reach; Matt was on his knees, the other Jan was being sick.

Green for the eleventh century. Jan turned, kicking the bundle as he did so. The tube weapon he could hold in his right hand, a little awkwardly, while he touched the pad. His left index finger stroked the green light. The familiar shimmering purple curtain appeared before him. He heard footsteps; the woman had regained her courage. Grasping the bundle with his left hand, Jan stepped through the Portal, and out into the centre of the Stone Circle.

1966 JUNE 22; 2.07 PM

On the dusty plain, the grass began to move. Swirling as if swept by a sudden whirlwind, it bent into patterns of interlinked circles. The shrubs swayed. But there was no breath of wind stirring the air, and the Sun still beat down from a clear sky. The vulture wheeled, attracted by the motion below, and dived to take a closer look.

In the underground chamber, as Jan stepped boldly towards the Portal, two more copies of himself appeared in quick succession on the other side. The girl vanished, along with her equipment, then reappeared, without the equipment, in the place of the man at the door. The lights started to dim, and a high pitched whine, on the edge of audibility, could be heard from the upper chamber.

Then, as Jan disappeared through the Portal, the whine stopped and the lights returned to a steady glow in the empty chamber. On the plain above, figures moved peacefully over the grass, enjoying the sunlight of a rare perfect English summer's day. In the sky above, puffy white clouds sailed serenely on their way, while skylarks swooped and dived in their endless pursuit of insects.

IT WAS, HE WOULD DISCOVER LATER, 9 SEPTEMBER, 1066. There was a brisk breeze from the north, with low cloud scudding across the sky, but thankfully no rain, at present. This time, he was not alone. Sheep were grazing among the stones, and scattered wildly at his sudden appearance. A shepherd, dressed in leggings bound with thongs and a sheepskin jacket, appeared from behind one of the larger stones, complaining angrily, but unintelligibly, obviously annoyed that his flock had been disturbed. Jan smiled, spread his arms wide, and shook his head, indicating incomprehension. The shepherd stopped, took a good look at the stranger, and backed off, still muttering.

I must, Jan thought, *cut something of an unprepossessing figure.* No wonder the team back in 1966 had put up such limited resistance; they'd never seen anything like it, never expected to see anything like it. Jan was no longer the sort of person he would like to run into on a dark night; he was, indeed, the sort of person who had frightened the shit out of himself—his *other* self—in a dimly lit room. He laughed, a little hysterically. If only he had a mirror.

The shepherd spoke again, in placatory tones, then turned and headed out of the circle, presumably to round up his scattered flock. *Pretty unprepossessing in this location, too.* In the short term, it might be no bad thing. A *deranged* priest might get the best of both worlds—freedom to roam about without everyone questioning the reason for his travels, and food and lodging when required.

The thought reminded him that his stomach was empty. And that after more than a month on the road, he was back where he had started. Worse—he had started, after all, from Winchester. Now, he was back at Sarum, near enough, and without a horse or a knife. But if he knew Matt, there'd be some ration bars, and a clean shirt or two, and another firelighter, in this bundle. And he still had to find out what this projectile weapon was, and how it worked.

Unless—the image surfaced slowly, as if from another life. MacNeil, standing at the door, with his back to Jan and Matt. "*There is an experimental weapon in the armoury. It fires a metal arrow, rather like a crossbow bolt.*" Who the Hell had they been planning to assassinate? This would need careful investigation; he hoped he hadn't damaged the mechanism by thumping Matt on the head with it. But no—surely anything out of MacNeil's box of tricks would be pretty rugged and idiot proof.

He lay the weapon down gently while he scrabbled the bundle open, began munching on a ration bar. It contained, as far as he could tell, almost an exact replica of the items he had brought back to 1366, except that instead of a waterproof folder of documents there was a flexible metal skullcap, wrapped around a bundle of six metal arrows. And this bundle, instead of being tied up in a robe, was wrapped in a heavy, coarsely woven blue blanket. Best of all, though, were the four green crunchy apples—his favourites. *Thanks Matt,* Jan thought; *wherever you are. And all I gave you in return was a headache.*

He paused for a moment, wondering. If this thing worked out, what he'd actually done was consign that version of Matt to the oblivion of the ghost realities. Matt Three, or Six, or whatever number he was, had never existed, and never would exist. But that hadn't stopped him being instrumental in the creation, out of solar mass energy, of this bundle of goodies for the benefit of Jan. The only thing it lacked was a good sharp knife. Of course, the coins were wrong for this location; but gold was gold, anywhere. Someone would be glad to change some gold pieces for local currency, at a suitably exorbitant rate.

Next stop Sarum, he told himself, sticking another ration bar in the chest pocket of the coverall for later, and re-wrapping the bundle. *A proper pack, a horse, and a knife. Then just let any of the buggers try to stop me.*

Not that he was unduly worried about being followed through the Portal. Somewhat illogically, he told himself that if nobody had come through right behind him, nobody was going to come through. If nobody came through, that was because his mission was going to succeed. And even if anybody did come through later, he'd be well on the road to Haestingas. They'd never see him for dust, so he would indeed succeed in his mission before anyone could stop him. He *would* succeed, because he *had* to succeed. This was his last, and best, shot.

Convinced, confident, and refreshed, he was off, striding out across the grass towards the track that he knew would lead to Sarum, crunching on one of the apples, and ignoring the little farmstead, warm inside his layers of clothing in the Autumn afternoon, in spite of the stiff breeze from the north.

EIGHTEEN

THE NORTH WIND AND STORMY WEATHER WHICH HAD greeted Jan in this location were, he knew from his study of the records in the Winchester Cathedral library in 1366, typical of the weather for almost the whole month of September, 1066. Harold, who had been elected King in January, on the death of his brother-in-law Edward the Confessor, the last surviving son of Aethelred, had assembled a great army and a fleet of ships along the south coast, in Sussex and Kent, ready to repel an antici-pated invasion by William of Normandy.

William's tenuous claim to the English throne was backed by the Papacy, something that the whole Catholic world would live to regret, but actually rested entirely upon force of arms. He would have had no hope of defeating the forces Harold had assembled at the end of August; but he was unaware of the forces opposed to him, and the north winds and storms kept William's fleet in harbour, preventing the two armies from coming to blows.

Within a few days of Jan's arrival, Harold received disturbing news that those same northerly winds had brought another invading army to the shores of England, across the North Sea to Scotland, from where they would proceed down the coast to Yorkshire. This, the last of the Viking invasions of England, was a force led by the King of Norway, Harald Hardrada, urged on by Tostig, Harold's renegade brother. With the wind still set deter-minedly against William's invasion, Harold moved north, swiftly, with his housecarles and other mounted men.

Jan proceeded east, rather less swiftly. Sarum proved a disappointment, muddier, more bedraggled and smaller than it had been in 1366. He was unable to obtain a horse at any price, and a knife (admittedly an excellent knife) only in return for half a small gold piece. With the rain returning in heavy bursts, he was forced to walk as far as Stockbridge, more than half way to Winchester, before obtaining a mount at the cost of all his remaining gold, leaving just the silver for necessities on the rest of the journey.

The horse scarcely justified the name. Where his previous beast had been a huge, lumbering brute, this was scarcely more than a pony, a shaggy, wiry animal, but one that proved surprisingly hardy. His feet were close enough to the ground that he had no worries about falling off; and although still no great shakes as a horseman, his weeks on the blanket on the back of his previous brute had made him competent enough. Nevertheless, it was only on September 12 that he reached Winchester, and only then that he was able to establish the date precisely. It gave him more than a month to get to Haestingas. Time enough, surely?

From his vantage point by the Westgate, Jan could barely see the wooden Cathedral, lost in the driving rain. *So*, he thought, *here I go again*. He had no hope of picking out the river or the land beyond, and no inclination to loiter, urging his diminutive horse down towards the huddle of houses near the Cathedral. No time, either, to visit the Cathedral, or do anything except rest up for the night, and press on in the morning. The most important thing he had learned from his journey over the route to Haestingas, either a month before or three hundred years in the future, depending on your point of view, was that delay was inevitable. Press on as far as possible, as quickly as possible, and if you arrived a few days early, all well and good.

The delay struck at Myddlehurst, two days out of Winchester, on Friday, September 15. Jan, who had been feeling tired and cold all day, stopped early at the cluster of buildings around the crossroads. He had slept rough the night before, and felt rough now. The sight of a long, low house, with smoke blowing in a streamer from the vent hole in its roof, was enough to persuade him that he needed to be warm and dry for this night, at least.

As he had expected, the long house was the home of the head man of the village, a steward responsible to the local Earl, Eadwig. The hospitality he automatically offered to travellers was as much, Jan knew, to ensure that he could keep an eye on them as to look after them, but it was none the less welcome for that. Inside, the smoke from the great log fire set him coughing, but it was worth it for the opportunity to dry out. As usual in this location, his formal Latin was less well understood than it had been three hundred years later, but he was picking up a basic grasp of the West Saxon dialect—enough to explain that he was on a mission, a Holy pilgrimage, and to ask for food and water, and a bed.

At least the communication problem meant he didn't have to go into long explanations about his journey; everyone was aware of the threat from William, and he wasn't the only traveller heading east in those days, saying that he was going to support Harold's cause. It was enough to ensure a reasonably warm welcome, in spite of the complaints from some of the older men about the difficulty of getting in the harvest with so many of the younger men called up to join the fyrd, Harold's army.

On this Friday night, Jan made even less effort than usual to take part in the conversation. He was soon rolled up gratefully in his blanket near the fire, still coughing fitfully, but too tired to care. But it would be a week before he would leave that room, a week broken by vivid hallucinations, in which he seemed to be far away in the north of England, and what seemed like lucid conversations in Latin, which, unlike the hallucinations, he was convinced must be dreams.

In these conversations, he repeatedly explained, to a patient, grey robed priest, that he was on a pilgrimage, a mission from God. That he must reach Haestingas in time for the battle on October 14th. And always the calm, grey robed priest told him to be calm himself, to gather his strength, perhaps to try to swallow a little soup. That if it was God's will that he go to Haestingas, then surely God would see that he regained his strength in time.

In typical dream fashion, he kept going over and over the same ground, never making any progress. But always, in between these dream-like conversations, Jan could see what was happening in the north.

While Jan lay in the house at Myddlehurst, discovering the hard way that his twentieth century medical precautions were not, after all, sufficient to deal with everything that the eleventh century had to offer in the way of disease,

Harold was moving north, less easily than he would have liked, slowed by the need to raise an army of foot soldiers to accompany his mounted force as he headed into Yorkshire.

The news from the north, brought by messengers with less and less delay as the gap between Harold's army and Harald Hardrada's narrowed, was bad. The Norwegians had crossed in three hundred great ships, carrying a force sufficient to overwhelm the northern fyrd. Scarborough had been plundered; the longships had moved into the Humber, rowing up as far as Riccall, ten miles south of York, the northern capital of England. On September 20, when, far to the south, an enfeebled Jan Ricardo was barely beginning to take notice of his surroundings again, the Norwegian invaders destroyed the northern fyrd, under the Earls Edwin and Morcar, in a fierce battle at Gate Fulford, just two miles from the city. As the Heimskringla Saga would later tell it, so many English were slain that "they paved a way across the fen for the brave Norsemen". It seemed that Harald and Tostig were masters of the North, and that the path south, to London and beyond, was open to them. Harald had himself proclaimed King in York, but stayed outside the city, with his army, negotiating with the two Earls over the hostages he would hold against their good behaviour while he marched south.

NINETEEN

J AN OPENED HIS EYES, STARED AT THE SMOKE-BLACKENED
ceiling. This was all wrong. Where was he? Where were the Norse
invaders? Had Harold already arrived?

He was naked, wrapped in his blanket, with more blankets piled on
top of him. Underneath, straw rustled when he moved his head. It was too
much effort to disentangle his arms from the blanket and move his body,
but even without making that effort he could see that he was in a small
room, with one door, concealed behind a hanging curtain which didn't
quite reach the floor.

Where was the fire?

Confused for a moment, he tried to sort out dreams and reality.

The fire, he decided, was real. He'd been on the road from Winchester to Haestingas, not from London to York. He had stopped at a village—
the name eluded him. Needed a warm bed for the night.

Last night?

Which night? How long had he been lying here?

Jan struggled to get his arms free from the blankets, raise himself into
a sitting position. The effort was too much, and he fell back on the straw
bedding. The contact between his head and the blanket he was lying on
felt strange. He lifted his one free hand to his head, felt the roughly hacked
remains of his flowing locks. *Why?* The fever, he answered himself.
Hadn't he read something about that? A primitive attempt to let the fever
out of a patient's head, by cutting their hair off. *At least*, he thought, as he
drifted back into unconsciousness, *they don't practice bleeding in this
location.*

When he opened his eyes again, the grey-robed priest was sitting on a stool beside him, watching.

More dreams? But no, it couldn't be. If the road to Haestingas was real, and this house was on that road, the priest must be real.

"What day is it?" He had to know how much time he had left. From the feeble state of his muscles, he had been lying here in a fever for days, at least.

The priest spoke, in Latin. "So, you are awake." He leaned forward, placed his hand on Jan's forehead. "The fever seems to have left you, Brother Sean, after all. And still in time to do God's work."

Jan realised that he had spoken in twentieth century English. He switched to Latin.

"What day is it?"

"Still impatient, Brother Sean? It is Saturday. The twenty-third day of September, in the year of Our Lord one thousand and sixty-six. You have time to get to Haestingas by the fourteenth of October, if God wills it."

The fourteenth! This priest knew—but how? Jan's heart raced, but he managed to stop his racing thoughts. No, this was no fellow time traveller, not another Matt, following him down the centuries. He remembered the 'lucid dreams' in which he had conversed with a grey robed priest. *My God*, he thought, *what have I done? What have I said?* But no wonder they had brought the priest to his bedside, if he had been babbling in a mixture of Latin, twentieth century English, fourteenth century English and pidgin Anglo Saxon. They would have thought he was speaking in tongues, possessed by either God or the Devil, and brought the priest at once to decide which. He might be lucky to get out of this without being burned at the stake. He had to put things back on a rational footing.

"I'm on a pilgrimage, Brother, I must . . ."

"I know. A Mission from God. We are all on a mission from God, Sean, each of us in our own way. But perhaps there is something special about your mission. Your visions, during the fever—if they are genuine, then certainly you must follow where they lead. And I must help.

"But you must call me Peter. Have you forgotten?"

Peter. The name brought back more memories of their conversations. Jan, pleading to be allowed out of bed, demanding to be set upon his horse. Peter, the quiet village priest, gently restraining him, telling him that God's will would be done. And Jan pouring out the story of Harold's march northward, the great battles to come, and the urgent need that he, Jan, must be there, in Haestingas, by the fourteenth of October.

How else could he know any of this, except in a vision? But why should a village priest take any of this seriously? Why wasn't he simply being restrained as a lunatic?

Or was he? How did he know what lay beyond that curtained door?

The effort to think made his head hurt. But Peter seemed to understand his concern.

"While you lay here in a fever, we have had news. Messengers from London, riding south to the coast, have passed this way. They say that Harald Hardrada, and Tostig, the King's brother, have landed in Scotland. That the King rides north with his housecarles and other men of the southern fyrd to meet them. They say that Harold, with the aid of Edwin and Morcar and the northern fyrd, will defeat the Norwegian invaders, while God's wind keeps Duke William and his fleet safely in harbour in Normandy."

So that was it. His fevered ravings had already been partially corroborated by news from the north—although the bit about Edwin and Morcar was clearly just wishful thinking. Since there was no way that Jan could have had information before the messengers had passed through, it must mean that his visions were genuine. And Peter was willing to take them at face value, in this superstitious age. Maybe attempting to explain things rationally would not be such a good idea, after all.

And maybe, also, he shouldn't seem too complacent about the news.

"So it is true."

"It seems that way."

"All these weeks, I have wondered whether I was going insane. And yet, it is true." He lay quiet for a moment. Then: "The messengers are wrong about Edwin and Morcar. They will be defeated, on the twentieth, before Harold arrives." Or had they already been defeated?

"What day is it?" he asked again. Somehow, the vital information had slipped his memory.

"Saturday, Brother. The twenty-third day of September. Too late, if you are right, for the northern fyrd. There is yet time for your own mission, though; but first you must gather your strength."

Lying back on the bed, Jan turned his head towards the wall. In the corner, he could see the bundle that contained his few possessions. Leaning against the corner of the wall was the long metal 'staff', with its heavy, bulbous end. Mentally, he ticked up a bonus point for MacNeil's department of funny tricks. Although the object was clearly something out of the ordinary, its clean lines and simple shape made it passable as both an aid to walking and a somewhat unusual (but effective, as he could vouch) kind of club, not arousing too much curiosity. He'd have to find a way to practice with it, soon.

He started drifting off to sleep, then became aware of a more urgent problem. Struggling to turn around to face Peter, he began to wriggle out of the blankets.

"Where is the privy?"

Peter smiled. "You will not be fit to go to the privy for some time yet, Sean. The privy must come to you, as it has done this past week." Rising from the stool, he turned to the doorway, reaching for an earthenware bowl, covered by a cloth, that lay beside it. Jan, feeling the sweat break out on his skin with the effort of even sitting up straight, silently thanked God that he had fallen into such good hands. If the fever had struck while he was sleeping out under the trees, alone except for the horse—it didn't bear thinking about. Maybe God really did want him to get to Haestingas in time. He started to smile at the thought, but the smile turned into a rasping cough. *Damn*, he thought. *How long before I can ride?*

He slept for most of that day, this time more peacefully, without the feverish dreams. On the Sunday, he was able to eat a little bread, as well as the soup he was offered by Edward, his host. The attitude of Edward was far too respectful for such a senior servant of the Earl towards an itinerant monk. Indeed, it was almost unthinkable that he should take an interest in the well being of such a figure, let alone offer him food personally.

There could, of course, be only one explanation. Knowledge of Jan's visions, and of his mission, was not confined to Peter alone.

And yet, this might be no bad thing. A fit man, riding hard, could get from here to Haestingas in a week. A recuperating invalid, liable to fall off the saddle blanket if he rode for more than a few hours a day, might be lucky to get there in three. And there were barely three weeks to go until the deadline. Without help, Jan might never make it. And his only hope of help was if the people at this location believed that he was some kind of holy man, a seer, driven to carry out God's work.

Well, that didn't differ so much from the reality, after all.

He made no attempt to discuss his dreams with Edward, or the wide eyed lad, perhaps ten years old, who poked his head around the curtain from time to time, checking, now that Jan was awake, on his needs. In any case, their conversation was limited to the most basic Anglo Saxon concerning eating, drinking and other bodily functions. But he resolved to take Peter more fully into his confidence, playing up the role that he had fallen into and elaborating on the theme that had been handed to him.

By Monday, he was strong enough to walk, with help, across the room, so that at least the chamber pot didn't have to come right to his bedside. He had discovered, peeping through the doorway, that this was a small room just off from the main hall of the house. Partly with the aid of gestures, he learned from the boy, Dunstan, that it was usually a store room, which had been converted into a makeshift sick bay for his benefit.

In the evening, Peter visited him again. Helped by the priest, he made it as far as the floor by the fire in the hall, where he sank gratefully onto the straw.

Peter had also helped him to dress, after a fashion. The long underwear was too much bother (he wondered, briefly, how they had ever got it off him), but he had on one of his own shirts, which somebody had washed during his illness, underneath a robe, belted with a sash, borrowed from the household. Peter had commented on the fine weaving of the undergarments, and their constricting construction; but he hadn't expressed any further curiosity when Jan told him that this was a common fashion among his people, far to the west (the Ireland story still standing him in good stead), and that he had seen many stranger fashions on his travels.

This story contained a large element of truth. Jan had found that the element of do-it-yourself required to keep the poorer members of society clothed at all led to a wide variety of make-do garments, among which his hardly looked out of place unless you looked very closely indeed.

By the fireside, given respectful distance by the bustling members of the household, they talked again about Jan's mission. He told Peter that

God had spoken to him in dreams, as far back as the spring, telling him that he must go to England, to be present at a great battle that would take place at Haestingas. He had resisted the dreams for weeks, troubled, wondering if he was going insane. Then he had gone to the Abbot, who had advised him to listen to the dreams, accept them as God's word, and go on the pilgrimage.

Peter agreed with the wisdom of the Abbot—but, after all, he had had what he could only interpret as proof that Jan's visions could foretell the future. He understood fully why Jan had kept the reason for his pilgrimage to himself, throughout his long journey, until this past week. And he suggested that it must be God's work that he should have revealed his mission at this moment, just when proof of its Holy purpose was at hand.

"But why," he asked, "must you be present at this battle?"

Jan shook his head. "I don't know, Peter. That is the thing that troubles me. I am compelled to be there. From what you tell me, it seems that there is truth in these visions, that they do foretell the future. But I do not know what role I must play in God's plan. I can see nothing beyond the fourteenth of October, and I believe it may be my destiny to die on that field of battle. But what role I must play before I meet that destiny, I do not know."

The priest reached over and gripped Jan's shoulder in a gesture of friendship and support. But he didn't deny the possibility that Jan's visions might be leading him to his doom.

"No doubt it will become clear in due course. But if Harold fights William at Haestingas in September, then surely he must defeat the Norwegians in Yorkshire very soon."

"Very soon indeed. The northern fyrd will be avenged." Jan said no more, and Peter respected his silence. But, perhaps because of the seed planted in his mind by the conversation, on the night of the 25th the dreams returned with full force, as Jan tossed on his bed of straw.

Travelling day and night, eating in the saddle, sleeping only when the horses needed rest, Harold's force had reached Tadcaster, on the river Wharfe, on the twenty-fourth. There, less than ten miles from York, he drew up his household troops in battle order. After a few hours' rest, on the morning of

Monday, September 25, he marched them through York, picking up recruits from the scattered northern fyrd along the way, and on to Stamford Bridge, where they came upon the Norwegians.

Harald was completely unprepared. He had no scouts out, never expecting that Harold would ride north at such speed, and was still negotiating terms with Edwin and Morcar. But although Harold had the advantage of surprise, he was still outnumbered by the Norwegian forces. The battle went on all day, and at the end of it seven thousand men lay dead, including both Harald Hardrada and the renegade Earl Tostig, King Harold's brother. Three hundred ships had brought the invading Norwegians across the North Sea; just twenty-four were needed to carry the survivors home. And even sixty years later, travellers would make detours on their journeys to marvel at the great heaps of bones which still lay on the battlefield, the only memorials to the prodigious numbers which fell on both sides.

Harold, and the survivors of his housecarles, had earned a rest, and returned in triumph to York. It was one of the greatest victories in Anglo Saxon history, confirming Harold's ability as a commander and cementing his position as King. But the triumph was to be short-lived.

TWENTY

DUNSTAN, EDWARD'S SON, HAD BECOME JAN'S CONSTANT companion. Like everyone else in the household, he clearly knew about the Mission from God, and held Jan in awe as a holy pilgrim. He was happy to help Jan in his still arduous, but increasingly lengthy walks—first within the house, then in the yard outside, eventually for a short distance up the lane and back. On these longer expeditions, any villagers they passed nodded respectfully, usually making the sign of the cross and mumbling some incomprehensible greeting at 'Brother Sean'. Jan got into the habit of making the Sign back, muttering a Latin blessing, which seemed to please them. He was happy to be appreciated—but did *everybody* have to know about his Mission?

On Wednesday, the weather cleared. The persistent northerlies at last died away, taking the rain away with them. A warmer wind began to blow from the south, easing the ache in Jan's bones, but increasing his anxiety about the delay. The horse had been well looked after, and by the middle of the week Jan was sure that he would be able to ride, at least for part of the day. And no matter how short a distance he could ride each day, it would be that much less distance to travel in the few days remaining before October 14.

But Peter, with Edward's collusion, still restrained him. Saturday would be soon enough to leave, he said. The last day of September, still allowing two full weeks for 'Brother Sean' to reach Haestingas in time. He would move faster in those two weeks, Peter insisted, than he would if he left now, before regaining a little more of his strength.

Jan might have tried to overcome their reluctance to part with him and leave anyway. He was sure that his status as a seer would prevent them from physically restraining him, although sometimes he wondered whether they still doubted his story. But they had a trump card. If Jan waited until Saturday before departing, Edward would send Dunstan to accompany him, at least on the first part of his journey. The offer was irresistible. Someone who knew the location, who spoke the language, and would be able to help in finding accommodation. Someone who could explain, in the right language, that Jan really was on a pilgrimage of great urgency and importance. Someone to help him on and off the horse, and to make camp for the two of them whenever there was no prospect of a roof over their heads.

And besides, it would be rather fitting for a holy man to be accompanied by an acolyte.

The offer was irresistible, and Jan waited, impatiently, for the end of the week to arrive. But while he was waiting, he had an opportunity to check out what was beginning to seem, in view of his physical weakness, an increasingly essential component of his still half-formed plan.

The change of wind on Wednesday, the twenty-seventh, brought feverish among the ships assembled in Normandy. By nightfall, a fleet of more than four hundred vessels was ready for sea, carrying two thousand horsemen and three thousand foot soldiers. The fleet set sail from St Valery, on the river Dives, at midnight, under cover of darkness; by nine o'clock on the following morning, Thursday September 28, Duke William of Normandy had set foot on the shore of England at Pevensey, in the county of Sussex. With Harold and his housecarles still far to the north in Yorkshire, William erected a timber stockade to protect his base, and set about ravaging the countryside, both in order to gain supplies and to force the English King to come to him and do battle.

Jan had picked the spot for his target practice on one of his walks with Dunstan. On Thursday afternoon he explained to the boy, as firmly as he could in his limited Anglo Saxon, that he wanted to walk alone, to try out his strength before deciding if he would be fit enough to travel on Saturday. It was natural that he should take his own staff with him, to provide support; the metallic skull-cap and two of the arrows tucked neatly enough inside his robe.

The air felt cool around his ears and the back of his cropped neck as he proceeded at his best pace (about half what it had been a couple of weeks ago) along the muddy track that served as the main road to London, turning off into the woods as soon as he was out of sight of the village. At least there would be no problem fitting the damn thing. He just hoped that his doppelganger really was an exact copy—or that he was an exact copy of the doppelganger, whichever way round it went.

He stopped in a clearing, perhaps twenty paces across, shielded from the lane by trees. The late September sun was breaking fitfully through the clouds, and there were patches of blue sky overhead. *Good weather for pillaging and plundering*, Jan told himself, thinking of Harold, still unaware of the threat from the south, enjoying his triumph over the Norwegians.

Jan checked his surroundings. He was sure he had not been followed, and there was no sign that he was being observed. This close to the village, the surviving wildlife was chary of humankind, and any woodland creatures must have scattered at his approach.

He had to loosen the sash round his waist, pulling the robe up to get hold of the arrows and skull cap tucked underneath the sash, inside the robe. His fine leather boots, now caked with mud, were temporarily exposed to view; they still kept his feet warm and dry, and they were already the envy of Dunstan, who helped him dress each morning, and who lacked the ability Peter had to hide his emotions. Jan had tried to keep his anachronistic clothing concealed from everyone except Peter and Dunstan, but there was no telling what tales were being spread, at least by the boy.

No telling, either, who might have gone through his belongings while he lay in a fever. But nothing seemed to have been touched, and any curiosity about the arrows had remained firmly in check—suggesting to Jan that nobody except Peter was aware that he carried them.

The skull cap was a perfect fit, as he had known it must be. He smoothed it over what remained of his hair. Trying to relax, make his mind a blank, he waited for the circuits to kick in. Always assuming that they hadn't been damaged by the time hop and subsequent rough treatment. Always assuming that he really was the double of the Jan this equipment had been tuned to—for it was inconceivable that MacNeil would have left his weapon set so that any Tom, Dick or Harry could operate it. It *had* to be tuned to Jan's brain pattern. But since he *was* Jan, indistinguishable from his doppelgangers according to Matt, that should pose him no problem.

A green spot appeared in his field of vision, apparently floating in space far in front of his right eye. A quiet voice seemed to speak inside his head.

"Rangefinder on."

He moved his eyes from side to side, then turned his head. Finally, he walked to and fro across the clearing, looking here and there. However he moved, wherever he looked, the green spot stayed in the centre of the field of vision of his right eye. When he gazed across the clearing at a tree on the other side, it looked like a spot of light dancing on the trunk of the tree. But he knew that it was an illusion, created by stimulating his optical nerves electromagnetically. This kind of control system was familiar enough from his training, although not in common public use in 1966. Time to try out the other half.

He picked the weapon up from where he had left it, leaning against a tree at the edge of the clearing, and carefully wiped over the bulbous stock with the cleanest portion of his robe. The whole thing was about five feet long. His right hand fitted comfortably around the stock, and his thumb rested naturally in a minuscule indentation, scarcely visible to the eye, on one side—on the *top*—of the barrel. *Made to measure*, he thought.

The only natural way to balance the thing was to hold the barrel in his left hand. He did so, pointing it vaguely in the direction of the tree he was looking at.

An orange spot appeared in his field of vision, dancing about as he moved the barrel of the weapon. The voice in his head spoke again.

"Weapon ready. Unarmed."

Holding his head as still as possible, Jan moved the barrel from side to side. The orange spot obediently followed, first to the left, then to the right. He tried taking his left hand off the barrel. The orange spot disappeared. He gripped it again, and the spot returned, followed after a split second delay by the voice in his head. The same thing happened when he held the barrel firmly in his left hand, and let go of the stock with his right; no orange spot until he gripped the stock again. *Definitely a two-handed job.*

Carefully, he moved the barrel until the orange spot overlapped with the green one on the tree trunk. He shut his eyes. The two coloured spots, just beside one another, stayed in his vision. No problem. The thing really could be used by a blind man, if he had someone to point his head in the right direction.

Opening his eyes, Jan reached down for one of the two arrows he had brought with him. The weapon *had* to be simple—foolproof for him to use, impossible for anyone else to use. And it had to be rugged. No chance of it being knocked out of kilter by being used to give someone a tap on the head. He doubted if it would mind the small streak of mud along the side of the arrow which he dropped, tail first, into the barrel. Where else, after all, could it go?

He returned his right hand to the stock, swung the weapon round at waist height, pointed it at the familiar tree. The orange dot had turned red. The voice, the electromagnetic stimulation of his auditory nerves, had changed its tune. Now, it said:

"Weapon ready. Armed."

The red and green spots were touching each other on the trunk of the tree. Nothing could be simpler. The controller took note of where he was looking, as indicated by the green spot, and fed the data into the circuitry of the weapon itself. Fire the thing, and the arrow would go where the red spot indicated. He had no doubt that the indicator spot took account of John Borodin's law of gravity, telling the user how high to aim to allow for the fall of the arrow during its flight. Briefly, he wondered whether his doppelganger had been intending to assassinate Borodin himself with the thing. Now, that *would* have been ironic! But the operator would have no need to worry about the inverse square law and parabolic trajectories. Look at what you wanted to hit, get the red spot over the green spot, and you couldn't miss. The only question was, how did you fire the thing?

He tried pressing down with his thumb on the all but invisible indentation. Nothing happened. He tried squeezing the stock. Nothing happened. He tried thinking his commands at the thing. Nothing happened.

"Bugger it!" he ejaculated, swinging the barrel upward as he shook the weapon in exasperation. "Why won't you fire?"

With a hiss, the arrow left the barrel of the weapon, pointing upwards at an angle of about forty degrees. He heard the rustle of small branches, disturbed by the flight of the arrow, and the *thwack* as it hit, two trees to the left of the one he had originally been aiming at, but he had instinctively blinked and ducked as the weapon went off, and failed to follow the line of flight.

As he looked up, a squirrel leapt from a branch of the violated tree onto its neighbour, and skittered around the trunk and back into hiding.

Dear God, he thought, *it's voice operated. Better be damn careful what I say when it's loaded!*

Carefully, he leaned the weapon back against the tree behind him, then turned, and walked slowly across the clearing. He could just see the end of the arrow, about two inches, maybe three, sticking out of the trunk of the tree, far out of reach overhead. The rest of the ten inch length of the bolt must be buried in the trunk. No chance of pulling it out, even if he had been able to reach it. Clearly, the weapon packed a punch, and would be effective against a man over a much greater distance than twenty paces. It was a pity there was no chance of getting that arrow back. Not that he ought to need more than one for the job, anyway, but you never knew.

Thoughtfully, Jan walked back across the clearing, picking up the weapon and holding it with more respect. *What the Hell. Better try one proper shot.*

Wiping the barrel and stock again, although he doubted that it mattered much, he reloaded. "Weapon ready," the voice whispered, "armed."

He picked out a spot on the tree opposite, deliberately looking high, where the embedded 'crossbow bolt' would be unlikely to be noticed. He picked the root of a branch, in the angle where the branch joined the trunk, and held his gaze fixed on the point while his hands, holding the weapon comfortably at waist level, moved it gently until the red spot was overlapping the green one. There was probably no need to shout.

"Fire," he said, in a quiet, calm voice, consciously straining not to blink in case he missed anything. The weapon hissed, and this time, through unblinking eyes, he saw the flight of the arrow as a silver streak across the clearing. It thwacked into the tree precisely in the angle where the big branch joined the trunk. Not *quite* where the green and orange spots danced side by side—but then, he couldn't swear that he hadn't moved his head and hands just a little while the arrow was in the air. Good enough, though. Definitely good enough for what he had in mind.

For the first time since he had arrived in Myddlehurst, Jan felt good. Really good. He still felt weak, but that no longer mattered. The cough was only an irritation, the fever had gone, he had a horse, a companion, and a weapon that more than compensated for his physical weakness. There was almost a spring in his step, as he broke out of the wood and turned down the lane back to the village.

"Brother Sean! Brother Sean! Wait!"

He turned, but he already knew who it was. Dunstan was running as fast as he could to catch up with Jan. He had, obviously, decided to follow his charge and keep an eye on him, whatever Jan had said about wanting to prove his strength by going for a walk unaided. The only good thing was that he seemed to have overshot when Jan entered the wood, and have gone further up the lane before realising that he had missed 'Brother Sean' and turning back.

A green spot seemed to be dancing in front of Dunstan as he ran. *Christ*, Jan thought, *the controller!*

In a swift gesture, he swept the skull cap from his head, crumpled it in his hand. Dunstan ran on, seemingly oblivious to the gesture. But still—*how much had he seen?*

TWENTY-ONE

B Y THE FIRESIDE THAT EVENING, JAN ENGAGED, AS USUAL, in conversation with Peter, the only person in the village who had a working knowledge of their only common language, Latin. The priest seemed strangely withdrawn, more reticent than he had been since Jan emerged from the fever, somehow wary of making a commitment. Jan, worried that he might be losing the support he undoubtedly would need to complete his Mission, tried to prod a sign of enthusiasm from his companion.

"Two more nights, then, and I shall be on my way."

There was no reaction.

"I went out walking alone, today. It was tiring, but I managed very well. I could probably ride alone, if need be."

"There will be no need of that." Peter made a visible effort to make a more positive contribution to the conversation. "Young Dunstan would never listen, anyway, if we told him to stay behind. He is determined to follow you, wherever you may go."

Jan couldn't think of a safe answer to that. Had Dunstan seen his shining skull cap? Or even his target practice? Had he told Peter? Was that why he had been so quiet this evening? But Peter's next remark began to make things clearer.

"So. Today is Thursday. The twenty-eighth day of September. In your dreams, you spoke of this day. Do you remember?"

That was it. Peter was waiting, to see if this part of his dream came true as well.

"I remember. Duke William landed this morning, in Sussex. Even as we sit here, comfortable by our fireside, he is ravaging the land."

"Should we warn the people?"

Jan shook his head.

"No. He will not come this far west. Sussex and Kent will suffer, for a fortnight. Then King Harold returns from the north, and puts the invaders to flight."

"Yes. So you have spoken."

Was the priest humouring him? Stringing him along until the weekend, when he expected it to be abundantly plain that no invader had arrived, at which point Jan would be denounced as a lunatic, or worse, confined and brought to trial for witchcraft and burned at the stake?

It didn't seem possible. Surely it wouldn't all end like that. After all, he *knew* what would happen, because it had already happened, in his own past. He had read about it in the chronicles in the chain library in Winchester, back in 1366. There couldn't be any doubt, could there, about the battles that had now taken place, in this location, at Fulford and Stamford Bridge, and the battle that would come, in just over two weeks' time, at Haestingas?

Hard though he tried to reassure himself, Jan slept fitfully that night, imagining a world in which Harold had lost the battle at Stamford Bridge, and England was about to be divided between the Norwegian King Harald, ruler in York, and Duke William, unopposed in the south. Or a world in which William's fleet had never set sail. Suppose, after all, that there *had* been another time traveller using the Portal. Someone who had travelled to York and tilted the balance of the battles there against the English; or someone who had taken advantage of the northerly winds to take a boat to Normandy, while Jan lay on his sickbed, and found some means of persuading William to remain in his own land.

It couldn't be Matt 2. What both Matts had said was clear enough. Matt 2 had started out as a ghost, and he would have gone back to being a ghost as soon as Jan had gone through the Portal and back to 1966. But if there could be a Matt 2 there could be a Matt 3, or a Jan 2, with plans of their own, coming back from some other ghost reality to tinker with the events of 1066. If anybody had been on his own trail, they would surely have caught up with him while he lay with the fever. But if somebody was interfering with events in the north, or over in Normandy...

143

There was a curious kind of circular logic to the situation, which Jan tried to use to reassure himself. If nobody came back, that meant he must have succeeded. As long as he was on his own, and knew the events in York and Sussex were working out the way it was written—would be written—in the chain library, it would be OK. It would be nice, if only he could bring himself to believe it. And he might find it easier to believe if only they had some reassuring news of William's movements.

There was another thought, which he tried to push to the back of his mind. If there was no opposition, that meant he would succeed. At one level, that was reassuring. But it also meant he had no choice in the matter. He *had* to succeed. Did he still have free will, or was he being carried along for the ride by inexorable historical currents? Increasingly, since the fever, he had begun to feel as if he was no longer the instigator of change, but a tool in the hands of—what? fate? A *disposable* tool, perhaps, once his job was done.

The uncertainty persisted into the Friday, September 29. Jan continued to make preparations, such as they were, for his journey. Dunstan groomed both horses, gave them more to eat than they needed, packed and repacked his own bundle of possessions, while Jan wandered gloomily around the house and yard, imagining all kinds of dreadful possibilities.

It was dusk when the horseman arrived from the east, dirty, disheveled, and with his pony practically foundering under him. While he gulped down water and they found him another horse, he panted out news of the great army that had landed at Pevensey the previous morning, and how Duke William was laying waste to Sussex. Then he was off again, on the last leg of his journey to carry the news to Winchester.

After he had gone, Peter came to stand by Jan as he stood at the roadside, looking after the lone rider. He placed his arm around Jan's shoulders, and spoke, softly.

"It must be a heavy burden to bear, Brother. Forgive my doubts. But even after the news from the north, it was hard to believe. Now, though, there can be no doubts. For me, or for you. God does speak to you in your dreams, and we will not further delay you in your Mission. Forgive me, and accept my blessing."

Jan came out of his trance.

"There is nothing to forgive, Peter. But your blessing I accept with thanks. It may be needed."

TWENTY-TWO

O N SATURDAY, THE WIND THAT HAD BROUGHT WILLIAM'S
fleet across from Normandy had died, and the air was still. The
early morning mist persisted, delaying their start as they hoped that it
might lift, but it was still curling about the trees more than half way
through the morning, setting off Jan's irritating cough as the pair moved
at a gentle pace out of the village on the road east. Peter, Edward and his
wife watched them go; a few villagers bowed their heads, made the Sign,
as they passed. But before they had reached the first bend in the road,
Jan, looking back over his shoulder, saw that a swirl of mist behind them
had wiped the village away as if it had never existed.

The two horses were almost evenly matched. Like Jan, Dunstan rode
effectively bareback, with a blanket for a saddle and his bundle of possessions secured to the horse's neck, in front of him. The boy took the
lead. He knew the road, at least for the first part of the journey, and although Jan had some idea of the lie of the land from his reconnaissance
in 1366, the track they were on now bore little resemblance to the relatively broad highway that it would become in three hundred years' time.

What with the late start, the mist, Jan's cough and the speed with
which his still convalescent body tired, they were lucky to reach Pulbor-
ough on that first day. Certainly not one fourteenth of the entire journey
they had to make; but the village nestled in the valley of the River Arun,
and they would have easy riding down the river valley to the coast the
next day. It made sense to stop, in expectation of an early start on Sunday, the first day of October.

Tired, Jan paid little attention as Dunstan made arrangements for their overnight accommodation. He wasn't sure what story the boy was spinning about their pilgrimage, but as long as it got them respectful attention, some food and water and a place to sleep by the fire in one of the houses, he didn't much care. What he cared about was getting to Haestingas before the fourteenth. If he did, everything would be fine, he told himself. If he didn't, what did it matter what the people he had met in this location thought?

He was, though, a little surprised when they were joined on the following morning by a youth, perhaps four or five years older than Dunstan, armed with a spear and riding a pony even more diminutive than theirs. His name, he said, was Ulfric, and he wished to ride with them to join the fyrd, to help King Harold sweep the Norman rabble into the sea.

Mentally more alert than he had been the night before, in spite of the stiffness in his limbs, Jan thought only briefly about the implications. First, how could he refuse? Ulfric would simply follow along anyway. Second, the closer they got to Haestingas the more trouble they were likely to run into. He felt like death warmed up, and the only effective weapon he could use in his enfeebled state had to be saved for one special occasion. Better to have an armed escort than not.

He shrugged. His Anglo Saxon was just about up to the occasion.

"Welcome, Ulfric. We ride together. Soon there will be a great battle. Welcome."

As they rode, Dunstan leading the way, Ulfric bringing up the rear, he managed, as he had not managed at all the previous day, to settle into the rhythm of the ride, allowing his mind to drift, ignoring the pain messages from his body. He knew they were making good progress; he had a pathfinder ahead, and a rearguard behind. Things were looking up again—if the progress could be maintained. His thoughts turned to Harold, and the rendezvous that they must keep. Still light headed, perhaps a little feverish, he could almost imagine that he saw what was going on, far to the north.

For four days, since September 27, the messenger had been riding north as fast as possible. Changing horses every few hours, he had eaten and slept, after a fashion, in the saddle, tied to the neck of the animal so that he could not slip off. Progress had been slow at night, and the late September nights were lengthening; but at least he had kept moving. Covering 270 miles in those four days, he reached York on Sunday, October the first.

It was the first Sunday after the great victory at Stamford Bridge. After giving due thanks to God in the great Minster church in York, the King was celebrating his success at a great feast in the city when the exhausted messenger was brought to him, stumbling as he tried to walk with legs that still felt the shape of a horse between them, and gasped out his news—that Duke William had landed in Sussex with an army as numerous as the fish in the sea.

Harold's reaction was immediate. He had moved north faster than anyone else could march to fling back one invasion of his realm, his surviving men were in high spirits, convinced of their invincibility; he would march back south again equally quickly, to fling back this new invasion. Although he sent out messengers to raise the southern fyrd once again, he had no intention of waiting for all of his forces to be assembled. Speed, he had proved in the past days, was all important. He would gather what men he could from the shires he passed through on the way south. The rest would have to make do without the glory of participating in the victory.

And so what if the defeated forces of Edwin and Morcar could contribute little to the army that must now march south? As his loyal subjects, the northern Earls must, of course, retain their men to preserve order in the north.

Harold's greatest fear was that the Norman invasion was no more than a spoiling attack, a glorified raid, and that after ravaging the countryside of the south, the heartland of Harold's own supporters, they would withdraw from England, taking their spoils with them, before he could bring them to battle. Speed was of the essence, for there was no doubt in his mind what the outcome of such a battle would be. He did not know that William, having moved his main base of action east to Haestingas, had already ordered most of his boats to be burned, so that his followers would know there was no turning back; even if he had known, in his present mood he would probably have acted just as hastily.

Harold's army, depleted by battle but toughened and in high morale, was on the move south again early on the morning of October 2, with messengers flying ahead to the ports, alerting whatever vessels were available to be ready to cut off the retreat of the Norman invaders, and ensure that William's forces would still be there when Harold was ready to fight them.

In just four days, the army reached London. On the outskirts of the city, Harold paused briefly to offer prayers in Waltham Abbey, a church he had founded six years earlier. There, those present swore that they had witnessed a miracle—when the King bowed his head towards the crucifix, the watchers saw the figure on the cross bow back to him.

The story spread through the ranks of his followers like wildfire. There could be no clearer sign from God that Harold Godwinson was about to win another victory. Morale buoyed even higher by the recognition of the Holy nature of their mission, the army proceeded into the heart of London, where at last Harold halted for a few days, giving his men the chance to rest and prepare their equipment, and to gather in such reinforcements as could make it in time, including the housecarles of his brothers Gyrth and Leofwine.

By October 6, Jan's party had reached Hleaws, a little more than fifty miles due south of London—due south of where Harold's army was hurriedly regrouping. They were no more than four days' ride from Haestingas, even at Jan's leisurely pace, and like Harold he felt it safe to take a couple of days to rest and gather his strength. The cough had got no better; his appetite was almost non-existent, and he had to force himself to eat a little bread from time to time. He felt cold all the time—colder than could be explained by the chill autumn air—and suspected he was running a slight fever.

But most important of all, he didn't want to get too close to Haestingas, too soon. Pevensey, the site of William's landing, lay almost exactly halfway between Hleaws and that destination, on the old pack road that they had been following; a detour to the north, through Horsebrydge, would be wise. But much of the land to the north, Jan knew from his historical studies, had been devastated in the past few days. Hleaws had escaped unscathed, and during the next four days William, learning of the arrival of Harold in London, would be concentrating his army further east along the coast at his new base in Haestingas.

Jan would rather follow them at a safe distance than stand any risk of getting swept up by the gathering of Norman forces and killed. At the very least, any Normans they encountered would steal their horses, and there was no way he would be able to get to Haestingas in time on foot.

Hleaws had survived the ravaging of the countryside largely because there was nothing there to ravage. The castle on the hill, of course, would not be built for another seven years, as part of Harold's fortification of the south coast to prevent further invasions. So the centre of habitation was still down by the river, at the point where the seagoing boats reached as far inland as the tidal waters allowed before unpacking their cargoes and transferring them to pack animals for the land part of their journey.

Only, there were no boats, no pack animals, and no goods in transit. The boats had brought news of the invasion, up the river Ouse, before William's forces had all disembarked; and the pack animals had provided the means for a rapid evacuation of the hamlet, westward and to the north. Everyone who could had fled, taking everything that they could shift with them.

This made life simpler in one respect. Jan's party had now grown to a round dozen, some mounted, some on foot but able to keep up with the small band at the pace Jan was travelling. They were not just eager to meet up with Harold's army in time to join the fight; they seemed to hold Jan and his mission from God in some awe, as the tales Dunstan told had grown with each day that they left Myddlehurst and the restraining influences of Peter and his father further behind.

It wasn't just that the story of how Jan had foretold the northern battles in his dreams had become common knowledge, and everyone knew that he was leading them to a great battle on the fourteenth day of October. Listening to the hushed conversations around the fire at night, with his improving grasp of the language, Jan had discovered that Dunstan had indeed seen something, that day when he had been testing the weapon in the woods. Not, thank God, the weapon itself in use, but the glinting skull cap, the controller, catching the light on Jan's head. Proof positive, to Dunstan at least, that Jan was a Saint. The story had grown in the telling, to become a halo of light surrounding Jan's entire head as God spoke to him (Dunstan probably even believed that himself, by now). Which certainly explained the downcast eyes and fervent Signing that all Jan's followers—perhaps he could call them his disciples, now—made whenever he was near.

Of course, these were a practical people. It wasn't just superstition that made them follow him. A known Saint, whose prophecies had already come true, was now prophesying victory in the battle to come. Good luck would surely rub off on them if they rode, or marched, with him, making them invincible in that battle, and bringing them fame and glory. And, of course, everybody knew that King Harold would be generous in victory, rewarding his loyal followers lavishly. The Holy Brother Sean would probably become a bishop, and would need his own household of followers; who better for the job than those who followed him into battle?

Jan made no attempt to disillusion them. He told himself that it would be pointless. Besides, he rather liked being a Saint. He got looked after—he needed a lot of looking after, weak from his illness and not really fit to ride—and it meant he didn't have to worry about being attacked by outlaws, or even a common thief. Who would dare to harm a Saint? He took to making the Sign himself with more of a flourish, and his Latin mumblings became more ornate. After all, he really *was* a sort of a god to them; a man from the future, with, by their standards, genuine supernatural knowledge and powers. A god with a mission, to change the future.

He no longer cared that much about whether or not the changes he made would resolve the ecocatastrophe of the twentieth century. All that mattered was to change things so that no more time ghosts could come back and interfere with his own life, to make sure that he, Jan, was the one who stayed real in 1966 while the others disappeared into the unreal time-lines where they belonged.

It wasn't much to ask of a god, simply to ensure his own existence. And with every day that passed without any sign of another interloper from his own time, Jan knew with increasing confidence that he *would* succeed. All he had to do was get to the battle. The weapon would do the rest.

This rag-tag group of disciples was quite happy to sleep in the fields, but there were enough of them now to begin to rouse resentment among the farmers of the fields they slept in and trampled over. At least here in Hleaws there were only a few very old men and very young boys keeping an eye on things. The fighting men had gone to fight; the women had fled, to villages beyond the range of the rapacious invaders. And although the old men and young boys might not be best pleased to have a band of a dozen fighters camping out on the river bank, and although they might at first take Dunstan's tales with more than a pinch of salt, there was absolutely nothing they could do except agree graciously to let the party stay for a couple of days, and offer to share their bread with Brother Sean and his followers.

Twenty-Three

T HEY SET OUT AGAIN ON MONDAY, THE NINTH DAY OF October, heading almost due east along the line of hills inland from the sea, through wooded country. The rest had done nothing to improve Jan's health, and he slipped in and out of a light fever as they travelled slowly, through a seemingly almost deserted land. The further east they travelled, the more the signs of the desolation that the Normans had wrought. Farms burnt, crops destroyed in the fields. Not all of the inhabitants could have been killed or fled, and no doubt they were watched from the forest and other hiding places; but they were too close behind William's concentrating forces for life to have begun to return to normal, and nobody was taking any chances with the small band of armed ruffians.

They reached Horsebrydge not long after midday on Tuesday, October 10. Smoke was still rising from two of the small group of houses clustered around the river crossing, and Jan decided that they were, after all, still too close behind William's troops. He found it difficult to think straight any more. On the one hand, he argued to himself, since he *knew* his mission was going to succeed caution didn't matter. They could ride on regardless. On the other hand, he considered, any self-respecting god ought to look after his disciples. Ride on now, and his band of followers might all be killed by the Normans, whatever happened to Jan. Surely he owed them something better than that? On this occasion, the cautious voice of reason won out.

Soon, he was almost having second thoughts about his concern for the well-being of his band. A dead pig, its throat slit and one leg missing, lay in a sty behind one of the houses. Jan's followers, proving their ability to look after themselves without his help, fell upon it with delight, and soon had it roasting over an open fire. They obviously cared nothing about the surviving villagers, hiding, no doubt, not far off, in the trees.

Jan, distinctly feverish, knew it was pointless to try to stop them, let alone to try to persuade them to do anything to clean up the mess left by the Normans. When it came to personal survival, they were all pretty much as bad as each other, it seemed, Norman or Saxon, as long as it wasn't their own village that was at risk. Well, if he'd had any doubts about his mission, that certainly helped to diminish them. He still felt affection for his own disciples, who had looked after him across so many miles of travel. He'd make sure they joined up safely with Harold's force. But after that, they would be on their own, while he went about his own god-like business of changing history.

He waited until the morning of the twelfth, Thursday, before moving on. His band was camped at the southern end of the village, and during their stay they had seen figures flitting out of the trees into the northern end of the village, doubtless collecting food and clothing, and departing again into the woods. There had been no point in trying to make contact with them. Jan and his followers were moving on, and then the village could get back to normal. If they didn't want to make the first approach to his band, he certainly had no wish to complicate things further.

Early on October 12, the King also set out on the road again. Although forty-six years old, no longer in the full flush of youth, he pushed himself as hard as he pushed his men. The elite of his force, the housecarles, were all mounted, and anyone else who could lay hands on a horse rode as well. But most of the seven thousand strong English army were on foot. Marching day and night, they covered the sixty miles from London to the coast of Sussex by dusk on Friday, October 13, scarcely a month after Harold had been called north to repel the Norwegian invasion. Those who had fought with Harold at Stamford Bridge on September 25 had covered the 270 miles back to Sussex in just seven marching days.

The last stage of their journey was through the forest of Anderyd to Caldbec Hill, a spur of the South Downs carefully chosen by Harold, who knew this region well. The hill was surmounted by a hoary old apple tree, an ancient boundary marker indicating the point where the three shires of Catsfield, Ninfield and Baldslow came together. It was an ideal rendezvous point, easily described to strangers, a landmark for stragglers to close in on. The hill was also strategically important. Just seven miles from Haestingas, it commanded an old Roman road which led from Haestingas to join the main Rochester to London road, the only route the Normans could take if they wished to march into the interior.

In spite of the success of his surprise attack on Harald Hardrada and Tostig, Harold was quite prepared to wait at Caldbec for William to come to him. Unlike the Norwegians, the Normans occupied a prepared, fortified position. But the Norman army, dependant on pillage for subsistence, could not stay concentrated in Haestingas for long; it had to come out and fight, or flee. Saxon ships now guarded the escape route over the sea, so they had to fight. And, Harold determined, they would fight on a spot of his choosing.

But in order to keep their exact whereabouts as secret as possible for as long as possible, Harold ordered his men to spend the night in the forest, ready to advance into position on Caldbec Hill on the morning of Saturday, October 14. They slept like logs after the long march, while William's men, learning from their scouts that Harold's army was nearby, spent a wakeful night preparing for battle.

Jan and his followers passed Caldbec hill on the afternoon of the thirteenth, several hours before Harold and his army arrived in the forest. They moved on a little way to the southeast, past the slopes at the end of the ridge where, Jan knew, the battle would be concentrated. He chose a spot beyond where he estimated the left flank of the English army would be, on a knoll by the road, just clear of the edge of the woods that extended further to the east. It wasn't perfect, but nothing would be perfect, and his hacking cough was now accompanied by stabbing pain in his left side. He wanted to rest. He wanted a warm fire. And he was inclined to persuade himself that by being openly visible he would ensure that he did not come under suspicion from either side.

He tried, in his clumsy Anglo Saxon, to tell his followers that they had reached the end of their journey.

"King Harold comes tonight, to the apple tree on the hill." He gestured towards it. "If you wish to fight, you must go to the King. Duke William comes tomorrow, from the south. They will fight on this field before you. I do not fight. I wait for God's guidance. You must go, now, to the King."

He wasn't sure how much of the message was getting across, but he was too tired by the effort of making the little speech to care. He sank down onto the ground, while Dunstan began to prepare the fire. The eternal woods might be gloomy, but at least there was no shortage of fuel.

After a short discussion amongst the men, three of them left on horseback, heading up and across the ridge to the old apple tree and beyond. Jan, wrapped in a blanket and huddled by the fire, eating a little of the food Dunstan put in his hand, took no notice of their departure, nor, initially, of their return, in the gathering dusk of evening. But the excitement their return aroused among the rest of his band could not be ignored. Hearing the hubbub, he looked up.

All twelve of his followers approached him and knelt. Ulfric, the first to tag along with Jan and Dunstan, spoke for them.

"It is as you foretold. The fyrd assembles in the forest. We go to fight, with your blessing. And tomorrow, after the victory, we will return to you, to carry out God's work."

Jan took in about one word in three, but it was clear that they were leaving, and wanted his blessing. By now, that was second nature, and if it made them happy . . . An impressive torrent of Latin, a flourished Sign, and they were gone, shouting to one another in their delight and excitement, doubtless to inform the gathering Anglo Saxon army that God really was on their side. He was desperately tired, could no longer think much at all, and wanted nothing except to sleep. But he wasn't worried. Any interference from his own time would surely have shown up by now. It hadn't, so his mission *would* succeed, whether or not he bothered to take any particular precautions over the next few hours.

It was as well that they left. In the small hours of the night Jan was prodded awake from a fitful sleep by the point of a spear. Sitting up in the glow from the fire, which Dunstan had been carefully tending for his sick master, he found that they were surrounded by half a dozen Normans, asking questions in a language he did not understand. He tried his Latin on them, telling them he was on a pilgrimage. They poked through his few possessions, taking anything edible, and laughing among themselves. He felt the four arrows, two concealed in each boot, pressing against his calves, and prayed—literally *prayed*—that they would not bother to search him. Perhaps his prayers were answered, for after a few minutes they remounted, two of them snatching the bridles of his own and Dunstan's horses.

The boy leaped forward, protesting, and was knocked to the ground by a single blow from the blunt end of a spear. Still laughing, the Normans rode off into the night. And if that was the way they treated a priest and his acolyte, God help the rest of the population.

TWENTY-FOUR

L ESS THAN AN HOUR AFTER THE NORMANS HAD LEFT, EIGHT
more visitors slipped quietly into Jan and Dunstan's modest camp
from the woods to the north. Their long, flowing moustaches identified
them as Saxons as clearly as if they were wearing labels on their foreheads;
but they were not particularly communicative.

"Come," one of them said. His companions picked up the few possessions that the Normans had left, including Jan's 'staff', and they were
escorted back into the trees and uphill, following behind the line of the
ridge, two of the warriors helping a stumbling Jan along.

This isn't right, he thought, vaguely concerned. *How am I going to be
able to carry out my plan?*

They were brought to a point near the apple tree at the top of Caldbec Hill. In a small clearing stood a group of housecarles, fully equipped
in chain mail, but not yet wearing their pointed helmets with the pro-
tective nosepieces. These lay nearby, with their long, almost man-high,
shields, rounded at the top but narrowing down to a point at the bottom.
The group, obviously a nobleman's bodyguard, surrounded a fair-haired
man leaning on the handle of a two-headed fighting axe, its head resting
on the ground. Next to him stood Ulfric.

Jan, gasping to catch his breath, aware chiefly of the searing pain in
his side, began to grasp what was going on.

Someone was speaking, but he couldn't make it out. He shook his
head, turning to Dunstan for help. The boy was used to his mangled
Anglo Saxon; he could halfway interpret for him.

"Who? What?" he managed to gasp.

Dunstan half bowed to the Saxon leader, tugged at Jan's sleeve to get him to at least incline his head politely.

"The Earl Gyrth," he replied, "the King's brother. He has heard of your visions."

Jan made the appropriate gesture of obeisance. *What a mess*, he thought. The story must have spread like wildfire amongst the fyrd once Ulfric and the rest had arrived, with their tale of a Holy monk who had foreseen the battles in the north and their outcome, a Saint who had led his band of followers to this precise spot, hours before the fyrd had arrived.

How could I have been so careless? If the Holy monk was also foretelling victory on the morrow, having already predicted both defeat and victory accurately, the excitement among the fyrd would be intense. All the history books said Gyrth was a good leader—he had offered to lead the fyrd into battle while Harold carried out his kingly duties from a safer place, and although Harold had turned him down the offer was taken seriously. And any good leader would seize upon any chance to lift the morale of his men, whatever doubts he might or might not have himself concerning the prophecies.

Jan spoke in Latin. He doubted that Gyrth, or anyone else present, would understand much of it, but it usually impressed the natives.

"I come on a Mission from God. In my dreams, he has shown me the defeat of Earls Edwin and Morcar at Fulford, and the great victory of King Harold at Stamford Bridge." They might not understand all he was saying, but the names drew a murmur of appreciation from the audience. "I have also seen the outcome of the great battle which will take place here tomorrow. The great victory of our King Harold Godwinson and his men." From the murmuring, they all knew the word 'victory', all right. And, after all, he *had* 'seen' Harold's victory, in the history books and chronicles. "I do not know why God wants me here, but here I must be. I want only to wait, and watch, and find out what God wills for me."

The last bit obviously went right over their heads, but now Dunstan was speaking, rapidly, in his native tongue. Jan, feeling cold and tired, sank down on the ground and sat there, huddled in his robe, leaving them to get on with it. Obviously, the boy was telling the full story, from the moment that Jan had arrived in Myddlehurst—a story even more impressive than the second and third hand versions that Ulfric and the others had been spreading.

At the end of his tale, there were murmurings among the men. Contented murmurs. The story was undoubtedly one to encourage them before the battle. Linked with the miracle at Waltham Abbey, it was further proof that God was indeed on their side. And Jan was beginning to think that they might be right.

Gyrth came over, placed his right hand on Jan's shoulder, and spoke something incomprehensible. Then he turned, and accompanied by his bodyguard set off through the trees.

Dunstan squatted beside Jan.

"He goes to see the King. We are to stay here. By the tree, Brother Sean, you understand? We can watch the battle from here, and wait to see what God wills for you."

By the tree. They would certainly get a good view from there, on top of Caldbec Hill, safely in the rear of the English army. But how the Hell would he be able to influence the outcome? It was all wrong; but he was too tired to worry. Still shivering, Jan fell into a half doze.

Shortly before dawn, the Norman army assembled into a marching column, some three miles long, and by 6.30 they were moving across the green Sussex countryside, in the light of an unusually bright autumn morning. News of the column moving north to meet him soon reached Harold, who decided to concentrate his forces on the ridge to the south of Caldbec Hill, overlooking the Santlache Valley. If William wanted to fight on ground chosen by the English, so much the worse for him.

The ridge was about seven hundred yards long, with forest behind it, and a gentle slope in front, down to a swampy valley crossed by eight small streams. It could only be approached across the marshy ground and up the slope, tiring both the horses of William's two thousand or so mounted knights and the legs of his five or six thousand foot soldiers before they even reached the English position.

Unlike the Normans, none of the English fought on horseback. They also had few archers, compared with the invaders. They would rely on the shield wall for defence, and their terrible close quarter weapons—axe, sword and short spear—to inflict damage on the enemy.

The bustle woke Jan fully from his dreams. Men were moving out of the forest and down the hill to take up position on the ridge. He reached for his staff, started to lever himself up from the ground. Instantly, Dunstan was by his side, helping him to his feet.

"The tree."

The boy nodded. It was, after all, as Earl Gyrth had instructed. He helped Jan over to the old apple tree, where he sat, with his back to the trunk, and watched the scene unfolding in the morning light.

Judging from the Sun (he had got used to judging from the Sun), it was about eight o'clock. He could see the mass of the Norman army, gathering across the valley at Telham Hill. Everything was in order, just as the chronicles had described it. Harold's army was hastily arranging itself down on the ridge. The two glittering banners, Harold's personal standard *The Fighting Man* and the *Golden Dragon of Wessex*, were displayed on the highest point of the ridge, while in front and for a good three hundred yards on either side the close packed ranks of his real fighting men settled into place, their mail glinting in the sunlight, jammed shoulder to shoulder behind overlapping shields, an impenetrable defence against any form of missile hurled by the enemy, or any weapon they might wield.

William's force moved forward and grouped itself into battle formation on the lower ground, less than half a mile below the wall of shields. Like King Harold, Duke William, seven years Harold's junior, fought alongside his men. They were grouped in three ranks, and three rows. With Bretons on the left, French on the right, and Duke William's Normans in the centre, the formation was made up of archers to the front, infantry in the middle, and cavalry at the rear.

Jan still had four arrows, two in each boot; he had the weapon, literally in his hand. He could probably get in a shot from here, hitting Harold in the back, before anyone could stop him. But the area to the rear of the English army was a confusion of camp followers, wandering horses, and latecomers drifting in from the forest and hurrying down the slope to take up position. He could probably kill Harold and change the course of history. But since he would, undoubtedly, immediately be killed in retaliation, there didn't seem to be much point. *No doubt Matt would have done it, anyway,* Jan told himself, *but I'm different. My mission is to make myself real, not to save the world.*

He thought about what Matt—one of the Matts, he couldn't remember which one—had said. Something about history being resistant to change. Try to change it, and it would act to minimise your influence. Like his counterpart, Jan Two. If you believed his story (and how could Jan doubt it, now?), he had changed history by publishing those papers about global warming. Yet the fabric of history had remade itself so that nothing much changed as a result. Jan had tried to change history, but it seemed to be remaking itself to write him out of the story, after all. Maybe 1066 wasn't a leverage point, after all; maybe butterflies could flap their wings here as hard as they liked, and history wouldn't take any notice.

And maybe it didn't really matter. The way he felt now, he'd be lucky to last out the week or so before the Portal pulled him back to 1966, anyway. There was nothing more he could do; better just try to keep tabs on what was going on in front of him. After all, he *was* supposed to be an historian.

He must have dozed off again, for the Sun was now higher in the sky. It was about mid morning, and the two armies were fully assembled, facing each other. A hush had fallen over the battlefield, and even the camp followers were quiet, watching and waiting.

Suddenly, a lone rider spurred his horse out from the Norman lines. A single foolhardy Saxon, oblivious to the need to preserve the shield wall, leapt out to meet him, swinging his axe. The horseman ran him down, skewering him through shield and body with his lance, then drawing his sword and hacking the man's head from his body. A great roar went up from the Norman ranks, and they surged forward, with a great cry of "Deux Aie!" (God help us).

It was all exactly as it had to be, exactly as the chronicles described. The English held firm, rapping on their shields with their spears and chanting "Ut! Ut! Ut!" (Out, out, out).

With the benefit of hindsight and a view from the gallery, Jan knew exactly what was going on. The screams of wounded horses and dying men mingled with the clash of weapons and the chanting for the best part of an hour as William's men tried unsuccessfully to break down the shield wall. His archers began to run out of arrows—on both sides, bowmen relied on picking up enemy missiles to replenish their stocks, and with few archers in the English ranks there were few incoming missiles for the Normans to make use of.

Soon, Jan knew, the cavalry would charge forward, intending to destroy an enemy softened up by archers and infantry. But the English had not been softened up, and the attack would be repulsed. The Bretons on the left flank of William's army would retreat in disorder down the hill, into the marshy ground below, where many of their horses would be lost. In spite of exhortations from the Normans, they would make no effective contribution to the rest of the battle, and while William's other forces continued to dash themselves unavailingly against the shields of the English, a steady trickle of reinforcements would help Harold to maintain his position. It would be a long day, a war of attrition, but at the end of it William would be fleeing back to the coast, where he would find the ships Harold had ordered into action ready to cut off his retreat.

Sure enough, right on cue, the cavalry charged forward into the thick of the battle. And, as Jan had known it would be, the charge was repulsed, turning into an organised retreat in the centre and to Jan's left, but into a bloody rout on his right.

But something was wrong! Instead of maintaining the shield wall intact, a large section of the fyrd, perhaps a tenth of Harold's force, broke ranks and chased after the Bretons.

Without knowing how he had got to his feet, Jan was standing, gazing in astonishment. *This hadn't happened.* The chronicles all agreed— the whole success of Harold's strategy at the Battle of Haestingas had rested upon the superb discipline which maintained the shield wall intact in the face of repeated Norman assaults. Those overconfident fyrdsmen would be cut to pieces out in the open.

Overconfident. Jan's heart seemed to have stopped. He told himself that it was just his imagination that suggested he could recognise Ulfric and one or two others of his former followers at the front of that ridiculous charge. But even if it was just imagination—*wasn't that kind of reckless behaviour just the sort of thing to be expected from an army convinced that it was invincible, sure that God was on its side?*

Jan sat again, head spinning, hardly aware of the charge by Norman cavalry which cut off the retreat of the over-ambitious fyrdsmen, and left them surrounded and fighting for their lives on a small knoll, to be hacked down and killed almost to the last man.

Perhaps he had changed things. Not by taking arms against Harold, but simply by predicting Harold's victory! Whatever the outcome of the battle now, it certainly wasn't going according to Harold's plan, or according to the chronicles.

Harold's ranks, though depleted, still held firm on the ridge. William's men retreated back into the valley. Both sides, as if in unspoken agreement, took time out to move the wounded back to the rear, to snatch a drink from the muddy streams, to relieve themselves.

It was afternoon before the fighting resumed, and now William had changed his tactics. This time, it was the cavalry that led the way, trotting their stocky horses forward and hurling javelins and other missiles at the English ranks. It was still a war of attrition; it still lasted throughout the afternoon. But instead of the Normans being worn down and forced into retreat, now it was the English, perhaps disheartened by seeing so many of their comrades killed, certainly reduced in numbers, who gradually, almost imperceptibly, began to wilt.

News was brought back to the group of watchers by the tree by wounded fyrdsmen, and by the occasional deserter. Earl Gyrth had fallen, slain (according to one messenger) by Duke William himself; Leofwine, the King's other brother, had also been killed. But if the stories were true, they seemed for a time to increase the ferocity of the English defence. Harold, fighting in the forefront of the battle, rallied his men, and once again the Normans were repulsed. But once again, to Jan's horror, at the moment when the English had achieved a respite and their enemies were in confusion, fighting madness overcame a large group of fyrdsmen, who rushed forward after the retreating Normans.

Even though his objective in coming here had been to change the course of history by bringing about an English defeat, Jan found he identified fully with Harold's army against the invader. From the vantage point on the hill top, and with the benefit of being free from blood lust, he could see with all too clear logic what must happen. Had they learned nothing from the disaster of the morning?

Somebody seemed to have learned from that incident involving the Breton retreat, but it was not the English. At once, William's cavalry wheeled, in what could only be a pre-planned manoeuvre, cutting in to the English and once again wiping them out.

Both sides had suffered heavy losses, but after this last fit of madness the English had visibly suffered heavier losses than the invaders. To Jan, sitting on the hill, it was now obvious that there could only be one outcome if the battle continued. The only wise course of action now was for Harold to retreat in good order, as he undoubtedly still could. William must be reduced to less than four thousand men actively able to fight, and he had no hope of reinforcements. The English could regroup, and deal with him later. There was no point in continuing the battle.

But perhaps Harold still believed he had God on his side. Perhaps he felt that it was his doom to follow his three brothers, Tostig slain at Stamford Bridge fighting for the Norwegians, Gyrth and Leofwine by his side today, into oblivion. Whatever his reasons, the English used the breathing space to regroup, and established the shield wall again, a little further up the ridge, where it was narrower.

The third great attack came late in the afternoon. This time, William used all his forces in a combined assault. The archers fired their remaining arrows high in the air, so that they would plunge down upon the English, forcing the defenders of the ridge to raise their shields in defence. At the same time, infantry and cavalry attacked, hacking at the unprotected bodies of the English. Grudgingly, Jan told himself that you had to admit this Duke William was a good general, not the foolhardy adventurer portrayed in the history books.

The result of his latest tactic was a confused melee of fighting, and for a time Jan thought that he had done Harold less than justice. It was by no means obvious who was winning. But as the light began to fade in the late afternoon, with the Sun sinking in a glorious autumn glow of red and pink to the west, more grim news came back. First, that Harold was wounded, that he had been struck in the eye by an arrow, but had pulled the missile out and was fighting on, like a wounded bear. Then, that Harold had been hacked down as he tried to fight four Normans at once, although blind in one eye and with blood gushing down his face.

But still the battle continued, with the housecarles of the Godwinson family still fighting around the standards, although all three brothers were dead. It was only after five o'clock, as darkness began to fall over the field of battle, that the remaining English, with no one left to command them, began to leave the ridge and seek safety in flight, under cover of night.

In the gloom, Jan became aware of Dunstan, horrified, looking up at him with wide eyes. The boy backed away. Suddenly, he turned, and ran off. The Holy Prophet, Brother Sean, the new Saint, had feet of clay, after all. His prophecies were worthless.

Or were they? Was it possible that it had been his prophecies that had precipitated the extraordinary overconfidence of the English, overconfidence that had tilted the battle against them in a close fought contest?

Leaning on his staff, trying to ignore the stiffness in his legs and the ache in his chest, Jan turned away from the battlefield and hobbled into the woods himself. There'd be no great abbey built here to commemorate the English victory now. There was no telling what would happen next. History had certainly been changed, whatever the reason, and his knowledge of the chronicles was no use any more. He had a week or so to keep himself out of harm's way until he was pulled back to 1966, and now he had every incentive to hang on and find out how things had changed up there.

Trying to think logically, he decided that William's only course of action would be to regroup in the Haestingas area, then head west, into the heartland of Wessex, perhaps striking at Winchester itself. So the best place for him to go would be east—or northeast, more or less, towards Canterbury. What better place for a travelling monk to be heading for? Of course, he wouldn't get there. He'd be lucky to get twenty miles along the way in his present state. But he might as well have a target to aim for, and a story to tell anyone who might want to know where he was going.

Still troubled by the cough, his body protesting but his mind in a whirl, he made what progress he could through the night. The big question he puzzled over was whether the change would be enough. If history really did tend to restore itself, would the defeat of the Anglo Saxons in one battle be enough to make much of a change, nine hundred years down the line?

After all, William's force was in no state to subdue the whole of England. Young Edgar, the Atheling, would be fifteen by now, and his blood right to the throne was stronger than Harold's—his very title, Atheling, meant Royal Prince, and in Jan's original history he had succeeded Harold in 1075, reigning until after the turn of the century. No doubt he would be proclaimed King by the council, and crowned before the week was out. Edwin and Morcar would send forces south to help the new King, just as the old King had aided them, and there were men aplenty in the west country.

The best Jan could hope for, in terms of changing history, was that William would see sense and return to Normandy with his life intact. In the confusion following Harold's death, he could probably get away unharried. With a young King on the throne of England, and William still strong, that would delay the English takeover of Normandy by decades. If he was *very* lucky, Jan decided, he might have gained the world a breathing space of a hundred years or so. And all he wanted now was to last out long enough to see just how much the world of 1966 had changed.

1966 JUNE 22: 2.07 PM

A sudden gust of welcome wind swept over the revellers on the grassy plain. Swirling like a passing whirlwind, it fluttered the long dresses and flowered shirts, and bent the grass into patterns of interlinked circles. In the sky above, the puffy white clouds took no notice of the ground-level breeze, while skylarks swooped and dived in their endless pursuit of insects.

In the underground chamber, the Portal was unattended. Everything was quiet. Then, a human figure, covered in a dirty blanket, appeared on the floor on one side of the Portal. Nothing moved.

On the plain above, the figures moving peacefully over the grass took a few dancing steps, girls swirling to send their skirts whirling in response to the breath of wind, enjoying the sunlight of a rare perfect English summer's day. In the sky overhead, the puffy white clouds still sailed serenely on their way, while the skylarks still swooped and dived in their endless pursuit of insects.

TWENTY-FIVE

JAN FELT WARM, FOR THE FIRST TIME THAT HE COULD REMEMBER. But the floor was hard and unyielding; something seemed to have happened to the straw on which he had lain last night, in the barn of the farm at Wye village.

He opened his eyes, saw the plain white wall in front of him, reflecting a soft, pink light from above; felt the warmth of the still air on his cheek.

So it does work if you are asleep. Wondering why nobody had woken him, he sat up, stiffly, and turned to survey the chamber. It was empty. The familiar rectangular frame stood in the middle of the circular room, but there was nobody else there, and no sign of a break in the wall opposite, where the door ought to be.

The staff was gone, of course. And so were the arrows, although he felt with his right hand to make sure. He stood, leaning on the wall for support, and walked carefully around the Portal, checking the wall for any sign of the door. He knew there wouldn't be any sign; that if he wanted to get out that way he would have to find the right patch of wall to lay his hand on, when it would open seamlessly.

Young Faulkner seems to have slipped up in this location, he thought. *But where was everybody?*

He looked at the Portal. It looked just the same, ready to send him back to 1666, or 1366, or 1066, or further, if he chose to touch the pads and step through. He shivered at the thought. Not yet. After all, according to Matt the Portal would stay open for about another thirty years, probably until the end of the century. Plenty of time for historical research later. What he needed was some good twentieth century food, and medicine. And it would still be high summer, here. The Portal could also send him straight through to the centre of the Stone Circle, in this location. He had no need to sit around down here, waiting for some member of this location's version of the Project to get around to checking out the Portal chamber.

That is, if . . . the thought was ridiculous. He couldn't have changed history so much that there was no Project at all, could he? No Matt? No MacNeil? No Faulkner to paint the hand on the door?

Whatever, it still made sense to use the Portal. Touch the right hand pad, step through, and he'd be out in the open air on the afternoon of June 22, 1966—the same day he had left, nearly five months ago.

He shook his head. The chronology didn't make sense, but he was hungry, thirsty, his back ached and he still got a pain in his chest if he breathed deeply or walked too fast. He certainly wasn't going to sit around down here waiting for Matt's counterpart in this location to get around to noticing him. Besides, he had to *know* what was going on up there—whether he really had changed things. Would he still find the semi-desert and blazing sunshine of his original location?

Only one way to find out. He stepped forward, touched the right hand pad, walked through the Portal.

Into a beautiful summer's day, with white puffy clouds drifting across a blue sky, green grass underfoot, a gentle breeze blowing around the stones. And people—*lots* of people, colourfully dressed in loose-fitting clothes, the men and women both with long hair, the men sporting beards and moustaches. There was music, coming from the other side of the stones.

He stumbled, surprised, trying to take it all in.

This certainly isn't the location I started from!

Somebody spoke behind him, the words totally incomprehensible, but the tone friendly.

He turned. He was being addressed by a bare-chested figure, with wild blonde hair and an impressive Saxon style drooping moustache. There was something odd about the eyes of the man—the pupils seemed to be almost non-existent. But he was definitely friendly. Jan listened carefully, hearing the words that followed, but failing to understand them, as the bare-chested man gestured at Jan's clothing.

"Neat gear, man. Really cool. But probably too hot, as well." Whatever he'd said, it set him off into a fit of giggles. Jan thought he'd caught the meaning, with or without words. It certainly was hot, inside this robe, a leather jacket, a couple of shirts and the rest. He needed to get rid of some of the clothing. He needed a bath, and a shave, and food. He needed to know what was going on—and most important of all, he needed to know if this really was 1966.

The man who had been speaking to him was now lying on the ground, gazing up at the sky, still giggling. Jan turned away, looking for somebody who might talk more sense. He seemed to have landed in the middle of some kind of open air festival, or party. There were young people walking or dancing around the stones, others sitting or lying on the grass, several of them couples engrossed in each other. Over where the track had been in the fourteenth century, there was a proper road, with a line of wheeled vehicles parked there, and some uniformed men standing alongside them. Some sort of authority figures, keeping watch on the festival. He decided he would seek information closer to hand, at first.

In the shade of one of the standing stones, a group of seven people were sitting cross-legged around one of the fallen slabs, using it as a table. They had bread, fruit and bottles of drink. One of them was smoking from a curious kind of pipe, the end cupped in his hand, which he then passed on to his neighbour. Underneath the bottles, on the stone slab, there was a large sheet of printed paper. The group looked a little more organised than most of the revellers. He decided to seek their assistance, and moved over to join them.

"Can you help me?"

One of the girls shuffled sideways, patted the grass beside her, smiling up at him. He sat down, to an accompaniment of friendly nods and mumbled greetings.

How could he ask them the date without appearing ridiculous?

"I'm lost," he tried. "I've been travelling. I don't know how long I've been on the road. What day is it?"

They shook their heads and laughed, obviously not understanding his twentieth century English. He was offered the pipe, but waved it away. *Imagine—actually inhaling smoke into their lungs! Could this really be the right century?*

A young man to his right leaned forward, spoke.

"I guess you don't need it, either. I don't know what you're on, friend, but it must be good stuff. Better sit here until you're straight."

The words sounded as if they ought to make sense, but somehow the meaning slid by him. He decided to try something simpler.

"Drink?" he asked, gesturing at the bottles.

Whether it was the word or the gesture, the message got through.

"Sure." The girl opposite leaned forward, picking up the bottle and pushing it his way. Jan took a swig. It was cider. He wiped his mouth on the back of his hand, leaned forward to replace the bottle, and noticed the paper it was standing on. There was a large picture of the Stone Circle, taken from the air, showing the revellers. Clearly, a recent picture. Above the picture, there was a caption: 'Hippies invade Stonehenge'. The printed paper must be a news sheet—it had news about this festival. He tried to make out the story underneath the picture, but the words wouldn't gel for him. It seemed to be English, but English through a distorting lens.

Then, one word seemed to leap off the page at him. 'Solstice'. The midsummer festival—June 22. That was what the Stone Circle had been all about, in prehistory. Did the people in this location still celebrate the solstice here?

The girl touched his arm, gestured at the paper.

"You wanna read it? We're famous—front page of the *Times*." She lifted the bottles out of the way, pulled the paper over, gave it to Jan. He ignored the words under the picture. He could try to puzzle them out later. He had seen something much more important.

At the top of the page, where it had been concealed beneath a bottle, was the date. Numbers were still numbers, whatever had happened to spelling and pronunciation. And the date was June 22, 1966. He had made it, back to where he had started. But there was no Project, no environmental destruction, and judging from the vehicles parked over by the road technological advance had been set back with a vengeance.

My God, he thought. *I did it.* But what had happened to the Project, to Matt and everybody else he had known? Was everything just a vacuum ghost? Was *he* just a vacuum ghost, promoted into reality by the Portal, borrowing energy from the Sun? Had the world he knew ever existed?

The Portal. It was still there, beneath where he was sitting. And it was, obviously, undiscovered in this location. It would stay open for another thirty years or more. If he didn't like it here, there would be ample time to 'discover' it, and go back to the past again.

The Sun was warm on his head, and the cider was warm in his belly. He turned to the girl.

"I don't suppose you know what happened after the Battle at Haestingas?"

She shook her head, still smiling, and placed a finger on his lips.

She was right. No point in trying to discuss things yet. At least, if the worst came to the worst he could surely find somebody in this location who understood Latin. But not yet.

He leaned back against the stone, and closed his eyes. He had a feeling he would like it here. The people were friendly and hospitable, there was no sign of environmental destruction, and he had nine hundred years of new history to study, once he could get down to the library at Winchester University. *Yes*, Jan thought, as he dozed in the sunshine, *I'm going to like it here.*

The newspaper, discarded by his side, fluttered in the breeze, several pages turning over before somebody put a bottle on it to keep it still. There was a boxed item, near the foot of the exposed page, headed 'Science Report'. Underneath the heading, the single word 'Aviation' was underlined, and below that was a headline: 'Concorde threat to ozone layer', with the byline "By Nature-Times News Service". The story began:

A surprising discovery has been made by researchers working at the United States space agency NASA. They claim that emissions from the exhaust of the planned Anglo-French supersonic airliner Concorde will destroy ozone in the stratosphere and allow harmful solar ultraviolet radiation to penetrate to the surface of the Earth . . .

Afterword

How To Make A Do-It-Yourself Time Machine

TRADITIONALLY, WRITERS OF 'HARD' SF ARE SUPPOSED TO *work within the framework of the known laws of physics as far as possible, but are allowed to make use of two 'impossible' assumptions. One is space travel at speeds faster than that of light, which is forbidden by the equations of relativity theory, and which no scientist believes to be possible. The other is, or was, time travel, which flies in the face of common sense, and is 'obviously' impossible. But in recent years, relativists have been forced to the uncomfortable conclusion that, in fact, time travel is not ruled out by Einstein's equations. This means that it is now possible to write time travel stories entirely within the known laws of physics, and you have just read one.*

In case there are any readers who may still think that the science described in this book is fiction, here is the English language version of an article of mine which first appeared in Italian in the sober pages of the science fact magazine L'Astronomia. The bottom line is that there is nothing in the laws of physics which forbids time travel, with all that that implies. The safety net favoured by relativists in our location is that actually constructing such a machine would involve very advanced technology. But that is a far cry from it being scientifically impossible (like travelling at a speed faster than that of light), and as Arthur C. Clarke once said (not Fred Hoyle, in our version of reality), any sufficiently advanced technology is indistinguishable from magic.

Scientific understanding of the way the Universe works, in the form of the general theory of relativity, has now progressed to the point where it is possible to provide you with the following simple instructions for building a time machine. This is now a practicable possibility, limited only by the available technology; we can accept no responsibility, however, for any paradoxes caused by the operation of such a machine.

First, catch your black hole. Do *not* try to find a black hole in the container in which you received these instructions. The black hole is not supplied with the instructions, and is not included in the price.

A black hole is an object which has such a strong gravitational pull that it wraps spacetime around itself, like a soap bubble, cutting off the inside of the hole from the rest of the Universe. To give you some idea of what this involves, imagine turning our Sun into a black hole. The Sun is about a million times bigger, in terms of volume, than the Earth. But in order to turn it into a black hole, it would have to be squeezed into a sphere only a few kilometres across—about the size of Mount Everest, or the Isle of Wight.

Nevertheless, astronomers are sure that black holes like this do exist. They can detect them by their gravitational influence on nearby stars— if you see a star being tugged sideways by something that isn't there, the chances are that the invisible something is not the infamous cat Macaverty, but a black hole.

As you are no doubt aware from your study of Einstein's equations, every black hole has two ends, and is properly regarded as a 'wormhole', linking two different locations in spacetime by a tunnel through hyperspace. We suggest that in order to avoid problems with spaghettification (see below), the black hole should have a minimum mass of about 100 times the mass of our Sun. This will make it very easy to tow the hole to a convenient location (such as the back yard of the Solar System, between the orbits of Mars and Jupiter) by dangling a moderate sized planet (you may find Jupiter convenient for this task) in front of it and moving the planet. The gravitational attraction between the planet and the black hole will then bring the hole along behind like a donkey following a carrot.

If you do not have a spacecraft capable of towing planets, we refer you to our leaflet 'Build Your Own Spaceship', available from the usual address.

It is now necessary to ensure that both ends of the black hole are in the same place, but at different times. This is achieved by driving your spaceship into the black hole, and out of the other end of the tunnel. After identifying your location from the star maps provided, tow the other end of the hole back to the Solar System.

You can now adjust the time machine to your own specification using the relativistic time dilation procedure. This involves whirling the second end of the black hole round in a circle, at a speed of approximately half the speed of light (that is, 150 million kilometres per second) for an appropriate period. The relativistic time dilation effect will ensure that a time difference builds up between the two ends of the hole. After checking the time difference from the usual geological indicators, to ensure just the amount required, you may then bring the hole to a halt, and your time machine is ready to use.

WARNING: We can take no responsibility for difficulties caused by careless use of the time machine. Before attempting to use the time machine, please read the following historical background and explanation of the granny paradox:

When astronomer Carl Sagan decided to write a science fiction novel, he needed a fictional device that would allow his characters to travel great distances across the Universe. He knew, of course, that it is impossible to travel faster than light; and he also knew that there was a common convention in science fiction that allowed writers to use the gimmick of a shortcut through 'hyperspace' as a means around this problem. But, being a scientist, Sagan wanted something that would seem to be more substantial than a conventional gimmick for his story. Was there any way to dress up the mumbo-jumbo of SF hyperspace in a cloak of respectable sounding science? Sagan didn't know. He isn't an expert on general relativity—his background specialty is planetary studies. But he knew just the man to turn to for some advice on how to make the obviously impossible idea of hyperspace connections through spacetime sound a bit more scientifically plausible in his book *Contact*.

The man Sagan turned to for advice, in the summer of 1985, was Kip Thorne, at CalTech. Thorne was sufficiently intrigued to set two of his PhD students, Michael Morris and Ulvi Yurtsever, the task of working out some details of the physical behaviour of what the relativists call 'wormholes'—tunnels through spacetime. At that time, in the mid-1980s, relativists had long been aware that the equations of the general theory provided for the possibility of such hyperspace connections. But before Sagan set the ball rolling again, it had seemed that such hyperspace connections had no physical significance and could never, even in principle, be used as shortcuts to travel from one part of the Universe to another.

Morris and Yurtsever found that this widely held belief was wrong. By starting out from the mathematical end of the problem, they constructed a set of equations that matched Sagan's requirement of a wormhole that could be physically traversed by human beings. Then they investigated the physics, to see if there was any way in which the known laws of physics could conspire to produce the required geometry. To their own surprise, and the delight of Sagan, they found that there is. To be sure, the physical requirements seem rather contrived and implausible. But that isn't the point. What matters is that it seems that there is nothing in the laws of physics that forbids travel through wormholes. The science fiction writers were right—hyperspace connections do, at least in theory, provide a means to travel to far distant regions of the Universe without spending thousands of years pottering along through ordinary flat space at less than the speed of light.

The conclusions reached by the CalTech team duly appeared as the scientifically accurate window dressing in Sagan's novel when it was published in 1986, although few readers can have appreciated that most of the 'mumbo-jumbo' was soundly based on the latest discoveries made by mathematical relativists. And then, like a cartoon character smiting himself on the head as the penny dropped, the relativists realised that this isn't the end of the story.

The point is that these tunnels, or wormholes, go through space*time*, not just space. Einstein taught us that space and time are inextricably linked, in a four-dimensional entity called spacetime. You can't, in the words of the old song, have one without the other. It follows that a tunnel through space is also a tunnel through time. The kind of hyperspace connections described in *Contact*, and based on real physics, could indeed also be used for time travel.

The CalTech researchers have shown how two black holes like this could lie at opposite ends of a wormhole through hyperspace. And the two black holes can lie not just in different places, but at different times— or even at the *same* place but in different times. Jump in one hole, and you would pop out of the other at a different time, either in the past or the future. Jump back in to the hole you popped out of, and you would be sent back to your starting point in space and time.

The time tunnel you have constructed using the above instructions *always* has the end that has been whirled around at half the speed of light in the future compared with the "stationary" end. Jump in the mouth that has been moved, and you emerge from the stationary mouth at the time corresponding to the clocks attached to the moving mouth—in the past, compared with where you started. You can set the interval of the time difference to be anything you like, using the time dilation effect, but you can never go back into the past to an earlier time than the moment at which you completed the time machine. In order to do that—for example, to go back in time to watch the 1966 World Cup Final—you need to find a naturally occurring time machine, or one built by an ancient civilization and left in orbit around a convenient star (see our leaflet, Locating Alien Civilizations The Easy Way). One obvious possibility would be to take a naturally occurring microscopic wormhole, and expand it to the required size using cosmic string.

Cosmic string, of course, is the material left over from the Big Bang of creation, which stretches across the Universe but has a width much narrower than that of an atom. Among its other interesting properties, cosmic string experiences negative tension—if you stretch a piece, instead of trying to snap back into its original shape, it stretches more. Any experienced do-it-yourself enthusiast will appreciate that this offers a useful means to hold the throat of a wormhole open.

HAZARDS: Please read the following section before entering the black hole:

1. Spaghettification

The kind of black hole astronomers are familiar with, containing as much mass as our Sun, would have a very strong tidal pull. What this means is that as you fell into it feet first, your feet would get pulled harder than your head, so your body would stretch. At the same time, tidal forces would squeeze you sideways. The relativists have a technical term for the resulting effect; they call it "spaghettification". In order to avoid spaghettification, the black holes that provide the entrances and exits to hyper-space should ideally contain about a million times as much mass as our Sun, and be about as big across as our entire Solar System. This is impractical at the present state of technology, but the hundred solar mass black holes we recommend can be navigated successfully, avoiding spaghettification, if care is taken to avoid the central singularity. We accept no responsibility for injuries caused by reckless driving.

2. The Granny Paradox

BE CAREFUL who you bring back from the future with you, and what activities they get up to while visiting your time. Suppose you use the time machine to go forward in time a few decades, and bring back a young man to visit his granny when she was a young girl, before his mother was born. The traveller from the future may, either by accident or design, cause the death of his granny as a young girl. Now, if granny died before his mother was born, obviously he never existed. So you never brought him back in time, and granny was never killed. So you *did* bring him back in time . . . and so on. WE DO NOT ACCEPT RESPONSIBIL-ITY for paradoxes caused by careless use of the time machine.

As well as the paradoxes, time travel opens up the possibility of strange loops in which cause and effect get thoroughly mixed up. In his story "All You Zombies", Robert Heinlein describes how a young orphan girl is seduced by a man who turns out to be a time traveller, and has a baby daughter which is left for adoption. As a result of complications uncovered by the birth, "she" has a sex change operation, and becomes a man. "Her" seducer recruits "her" into the time service, and reveals that he is in fact "her" older self. The baby, which the older version has meanwhile taken back in time to the original orphanage, is a younger version of both of them. The closed loop is delightful, and, we are now told, violates no known laws of physics—although the biology involved is decidedly implausible. WE DO NOT ACCEPT RESPONSIBILITY for travellers stuck in time loops.

And now, you are ready to enjoy decades of harmless amusement with your time machine. In the event of difficulties, please do not hesitate to contact our customer service department, which is located at the usual address, and in the year 4242 AD.

DEEP SCIENCE: Readers interested in the scientific theory underlying time machine construction, rather than just the practical aspects, may be interested to know something of current black hole research. Quite apart from the large black holes you would need to build a working time machine, the equations say that the Universe may be full of absolutely tiny black holes, each much smaller than an atom. These black holes might make up the very structure of "empty space" itself. Because they are so small, nothing material could ever fall in to such a "microscopic" black hole—if your mouth is smaller than an atom, there is very little you can feed on. But if the theory is right, these microscopic wormholes may provide a network of hyperspace connections which links every point in space and time with every other point in space and time.

This could be very useful, because one of the deep mysteries of the Universe is how every bit of the Universe knows what the laws of physics are. Consider an electron. All electrons have exactly the same mass, and exactly the same electric charge. This is true of electrons here on Earth, and studies of the spectrum of light from distant stars show that it is also true of electrons in galaxies millions of light years away, on the other side of the Universe. But how do all these electrons "know" what charge and mass they ought to have? If no signal can travel faster than light (which is certainly true, many experiments have confirmed, in ordinary space), how do electrons here on Earth and those in distant galaxies relate to each other and make sure they all have identical properties?

The answer may lie in all those myriads of microscopic black holes and tiny wormhole connections through hyperspace. Nothing *material* can travel through a microscopic wormhole—but maybe information (the laws of physics) can leak through the wormholes, spreading instantaneously to every part of the universe and every point in time to ensure that all the electrons, all the atoms and everything that they are made of and that they make up obeys the same physical laws.

And there you have the ultimate paradox. It may be that we only actually have universal laws of physics *because* time travel is possible. In which case, it is hardly surprising that the laws of physics permit time travel.

John Gribbin

For more about black holes in general, cosmic string, and time travel in particular, see:

John Gribbin, *In Search of the Edge of Time* (US title *Unveiling the Edge of Time*), Penguin, London and Harmony, New York.

John and Mary Gribbin, *Time & Space*, Dorling Kindersley, London.

Kip Thorne, *Black Holes and Time Warps*, Norton, New York, and Picador, London.